PRAISE FOR *LIVING DEAD GIRL*

☆ "Disturbing but fascinating, the book exerts an inescapable grip on readers."   —*PW*, starred review

☆ "Searing and heartbreaking."   —*BCCB*, starred review

☆ "Scott gives the phrase 'emotionally wrenching' a whole new meaning in this searing book."   —*Booklist*, starred review

"Scott's spare language . . . is powerful, gripping, and heart-wrenching. The final page will leave you stunned."   —TeenReads.com

"Scott's novel is repellent in exact proportion to the brilliance of its execution."   —*Horn Book*

"Some books are read and put away. Others demand to be talked about. Elizabeth Scott's *Living Dead Girl* will be talked about."
—Ellen Hopkins, *New York Times* bestselling author of *Crank*

"Most authors want to hear 'I couldn't put it down' from their fans. *Living Dead Girl* is a book you *have* to put down; then you have to pick it right back up. The beauty of this story is that, though none of its readers will have had this experience, all will feel connected to it."
—Chris Crutcher, author of *Staying Fat for Sarah Byrnes* and *Deadline*

"A haunting story of an abducted girl you'll be desperate and helpless to save; her captor so disturbing, so menacing, you'll want to claw the pages from this book and shred them."
—Lisa McMann, *New York Times* bestselling author of *Wake* and *Fade*

A 2009 ALA BEST BOOK FOR YOUNG ADULTS ♦ A 2009 ALA QUICK PICK FOR RELUCTANT READERS ♦ A 2009 ALA TEENS' TOP TEN NOMINEE ♦ A 2009 AMELIA BLOOMER PROJECT YOUNG ADULT FICTION PICK ♦ A 2009 NYPL STUFF FOR THE TEEN AGE SELECTION ♦ A 2008 *BCCB* BLUE RIBBON AWARD WINNER ♦ A 2008 *VOYA* EDITOR'S CHOICE FOR TEENS ♦ A 2008 ABC BEST BOOKS FOR CHILDREN TEEN SELECTION ♦ A TEENREADS.COM BEST BOOK OF 2008

Also by **ELIZABETH SCOTT**

Bloom
Perfect You
Something, Maybe

living
dead
girl

ELIZABETH SCOTT

Simon Pulse

NEW YORK | LONDON | TORONTO | SYDNEY

SIMON PULSE

An imprint of Simon & Schuster Children's Publishing Division

1230 Avenue of the Americas, New York, NY 10020

Copyright © 2008 by Elizabeth Spencer

All rights reserved, including the right of reproduction
in whole or in part in any form.

SIMON PULSE and colophon are registered trademarks of Simon & Schuster, Inc.

Also available in a Simon Pulse hardcover edition.

For information about special discounts for bulk purchases, please contact
Simon & Schuster Special Sales at 1-866-506-1949 or business@simonandschuster.com.

The Simon & Schuster Speakers Bureau can bring authors to your live event. For more
information or to book an event contact the Simon & Schuster Speakers Bureau
at 1-866-248-3049 or visit our website at www.simonspeakers.com.

Designed by Mike Rosamilia

The text of this book was set in Adobe Garamond.

Manufactured in the United States of America

4 6 8 10 9 7 5 3

Library of Congress Control Number 2007943736

ISBN: 978-1-4169-6059-1 (hc)

ISBN: 978-1-4169-6060-7 (pbk)

THANKS TO Jennifer Klonsky for championing this book; to Bethany Buck, Paul Crichton, Russell Gordon, Victor Iannone, Lucille Rettino, Michael del Rosario, Kelly Stocks, and everyone else at Simon Pulse for all their support; and to Robin Rue, who is always in my corner.

Thanks also go to Katharine Beutner, Jessica Brearton, Diana Fox, and Amy Pascale for their encouragement and kindness.

And finally, Shana Naomi Krochmal—thank you for urging me to do more with this than leave it sitting on my hard drive. This book wouldn't be here without you.

1

THIS IS HOW THINGS LOOK:

Shady Pines Apartments, four shabby buildings tucked off the road near the highway. Across from a strip mall with nail places and a cash-loan store that advertises on TV all the time. There's also a drugstore and tiny restaurants, every one opening and closing within months.

Shady Pines is nice enough, if it's all you can afford. The stairs are chipped but solid, the washing machines always work, and management picks up the trash once a week.

A few mothers sit outside their buildings, resting in fraying lawn chairs and talking over each other while their children run around, playing. One dog lies sleeping in the sun, twitching its tail when a child comes over and pats the top of its head before running away, giggling.

That man in the far building, the car guy, is outside, a pile of parts scattered on the black ooze of the parking lot around him. Car guy has been here since you moved in, but you never see him except for sunny weekends, when he works on his car.

Not that he ever drives it.

He's a strange one, that's for sure, living alone, always with that car, not really ever talking to anyone, but every place has one weirdo, and at least car guy cleans up after himself. He's almost obsessive about it.

Still, see how he sighs when that man, the one whose daughter is quiet and, sadly, a little slow, pulls into the space next to his? See how he watches the girl get out of the car? She's a skinny little thing, always hunching over a bit, like she's taller than she thinks she is. Homeschooled, of course, because of how she is, or so someone once told you when you were getting the mail, and there are no secrets around here, not with everyone living so close together.

She walks slowly across the lot, trailing behind her father, who waits patiently for her to get to the building door, holding it open even though he's carrying all the bags. She doesn't even say thank you, but what can you expect? Kids never know how good they have it.

2

T HIS IS HOW THINGS ARE:

Cold, from the grocery store, from the dairy aisle you walked down to pick up the yogurt, from the frozen-food aisle, its cases filled deep with frozen pizzas and ice cream in large round containers.

Cold, getting out of the truck, foot clinking over something metallic, piece of a car lying on the ground.

Don't stop to look.

Walk up the stairs, Ray's footsteps behind you. Listen to him pause, smiling at the one open apartment door, the Indian family on the second floor, always children running in and out, sometimes their TV turned up so loud at night Ray has to go down there and knock on the door, say please turn it down? Thank you so much.

"Was that guy in the parking lot looking at you?" Ray says when you walk into the apartment, as soon as the door thunks closed and he's turned the locks, one, two, three. Better safe than sorry, he always says.

Shake your head no, no. Even if he did look, it would never be at you.

No one ever really looks at you.

Ray puts the groceries away, yogurt in the fridge, his oatmeal in its individual packets in the cabinet above the sink. Five apples, one for each day when he comes home from work. Five TV dinners you'll heat up at night for him to eat unless he brings something home.

He comes over to the sofa. Holds out a glass of water so cold the sides are frosty, ice cubes clinking inside. You've pulled your skirt up to your waist, arms resting by your sides, palms up and open. Waiting.

"Good," he says, and lies on top of you. Heavy and pushing, always pushing. "Good girl, Alice."

Afterward, he will give you the water and a container of yogurt. He will sit with one hand curled around your knee. You will watch TV together. He will tell you how lucky you are.

"Yes," you will say. "I know I am."

3

ONCE UPON A TIME, I DID NOT LIVE in Shady Pines.

Once upon a time, my name was not Alice.

Once upon a time, I didn't know how lucky I was.

5

4

I EAT FOURTEEN CHOCOLATE-HAZELNUT candies, round and wrapped in silver foil that crackles when I snap it open.

I also eat six cookies, long brittle tubes filled with chocolate; one puffy cheesy thing that tastes old, all grease and bitterness; and two mints before a woman in a sky blue shirt comes out and calls my name.

The women I'm sitting with, all older, all reading magazines that promise quick dinners and happier children, look relieved.

They've noticed the pile of wrappers around me, noticed how I sat and ate while they sipped diet sodas or water and gave each other cautious looks if they reached near the candy when grabbing another magazine.

They know I do not belong here, that there is something not quite right about me.

But they will do nothing about it. They will say nothing, ask no questions. No one does. No one has.

No one ever will.

"Alice?" the woman in the sky blue shirt asks again, and I stand up, swallowing a last bit of cookie. Flour and sugar, brittle sweet.

There is a plastic decoration on the wall across from me; clear rippled plastic resting against a blue wall. A reverse ocean, with no water for anyone to drown in.

I can see myself in the plastic and it waves me into a strange, distorted creature, the shadow of something or someone.

I look wrong.

I look dead.

I'm not, though. I'm only partway there, a living dead girl.

I have been for five years.

5

ONCE UPON A TIME, THERE WAS A little girl. She lived in a town four hours away from here, in a house on a street named Daisy Lane. She had a mother and a father and her own room and a TV and sometimes could stay up late to watch movies on the weekend if she ate all her dinner.

She had a cat and three best friends and wanted to work with dolphins. She had posters of them on her walls, and her computer screen saver was one, a dolphin with warm eyes and a sweet grin gleaming out at you. All her stuffed animals, except for the stupid ones her grandparents gave her, were dolphins.

One day she went to the aquarium. She wore blue

jeans, a white shirt (no logos, no designs), and sneakers (white, with white socks). She went with her fifth-grade class, and since it was three days before her tenth birthday, she thought her friends would let her sit by the window on the bus.

They didn't, and when they got to the aquarium there weren't any dolphins and her friends got mad because she wouldn't loan them her lip gloss—it was new, it tasted like cream soda, and she didn't want to share.

She was a selfish little girl.

She paid for it.

6

"DAY OFF FROM SCHOOL?" SOMEONE asks, and I realize the woman with the sky blue shirt is gone and I've been guided into a room where another woman stands, smiling and ready.

"Skipping," I say, stripping off my clothes, down to one of Ray's old T-shirts. Smell of him all around me, always.

"I used to do that," the woman says, smiling more, like we share a secret. She has a mole on her face with two hairs growing out of it. You'd think she'd notice a thing like that.

"Ready," I say, lying down, and the woman motions for me to spread my legs.

"You want it all gone?"

I nod.

She is supposed to ask how old I am, and maybe other things. Something. There is a sign out front that says minors must have a parent or guardian present to sign off on all services, and this isn't a desperate, dying store that needs customers. This is a busy, bright place, where women wait and there is a girl whose only job is to ask you if you want anything to drink. (Coffee? Water? Diet soda?)

It doesn't matter, though. The woman standing over me won't ask any questions. She never does. Never has.

Never will.

She starts to wax. My eyes burn and then water as she rips hair away, stripping my flesh.

It is good for women to look like little girls now, to have no hair between their legs. The women out in the waiting room, the ones who will not look at me, are here for that too, to be made into smooth, hairless creatures.

They will have their skin polished, smoothed, so everyone can pretend they are young again.

Everyone wants the young.

7

ONCE UPON A TIME, THERE WAS A girl in an aquarium.

She wouldn't share her lip gloss and so her friends said she couldn't walk with them.

She got mad and went off to look at the penguins, which weren't dolphins but looked pretty, like in the movies she'd seen with her mother and father. Her lips tasted like cream soda, but she actually didn't like it all that much (it was the only flavor left and her mother had agreed to buy her lip gloss once, just this once, and she knew she had to take what she could get) and she missed her friends.

Plus the penguins got boring fast. They just stood around looking like they knew they weren't in a real home. Looking like they knew their lives were just a lie.

A man tapped her shoulder and told her she needed to go find her class, that they were watching a movie.

"It's already started," he said. "You better hurry up."

"Oh," the girl said. "Where?"

"The movie theater."

The girl looked at him blankly. She didn't know where that was. They'd been given maps when they came in, but she and her friends hadn't looked at them. They were bright red with stupid baby-looking arrows drawn on them to show where you were when you got the map. Dumb. Like they didn't know where they were?

They balled them up and threw them away. Then she wouldn't loan them her lip gloss.

Then she was alone.

The man sighed. "Fine, I'll show you. Come with me."

The girl knew she wasn't supposed to go anywhere with strangers, but the man had on a blue shirt like everyone who worked at the aquarium, and he was crabby like the lady who'd told them welcome and to be quiet in the same sentence. He was just an annoying, boring grown-up, not like the strangers she was warned about, who spoke sweetly creepy, things like oh little girl, come sit on my lap, or offered rides or candy or secrets.

The man took her outside, because her class was in the other building, the new one. She'd seen it as she came in, and had wondered why they'd put in a movie theater but not dolphins.

Before they went outside, before they even left the penguins (who were still just standing there, doing nothing, like they were watching them), he gave her a baseball cap.

"Everyone got one," he said. "Yours is the only one left, though, so it's too big. Better tuck your hair up under it. Maybe that way it'll stay on."

So the girl mashed her hair up under the hat so the hat wouldn't fall off and went outside. When she did, the man stayed behind to say something to the woman at the door. Grown-ups and all their boring talk.

8

"ALL RIGHT, ALICE," THE WOMAN RIPPING off my flesh says. "You can get up now. We're done."

9

THE GIRL WENT OUTSIDE AND THE man caught up to her in three easy steps. She heard him coming—one step, two step, three—and sighed, eager to get back to her friends.

"This way," he said, and she followed.

"Sorry I had to stop for a second there," he said as they walked. "I had to ask the lady by the door where the gift shop was. She thought you were my little boy. Isn't that funny? You don't look like a boy at all."

10

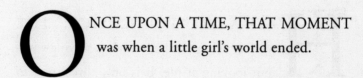

O NCE UPON A TIME, THAT MOMENT was when a little girl's world ended.

11

"HAVE A GREAT DAY, ALICE," THE woman tells me as I am leaving, waving without looking at me. It is only three steps to leave her behind, the door to her little room with its light and wax and hot pain.

Ray says it's sad how women try so hard to be young, to pretend they are something they have forgotten.

"You can never remember the best part of yourself when you grow up, Alice," he tells me. "My mother told me that, and it's true. So what do you do?"

12

NEVER GROW UP.

Like something out of a story, maybe.

Try saying it while a hot, heavy hand pinches, testing to make sure you're still child enough.

Try saying it when you can't grow, when you're forever trapped where someone else wants you to be.

13

GET UP.

Those were the first words I ever heard.

Open my eyes, see a girl, black and blue all over, dried blood along her thighs. Red brown stains smeared across the hairless juncture between.

"Get up and take a bath, Alice," the man in the blue shirt said, and Alice did.

I did.

That's how I was born. Naked, hairless, covered in blood like all babies.

Named, bathed, and then taken out into the world.

14

I PAY FOR MY WAXING AND WAIT FOR my receipt. The woman who prints it out asks if I want to leave a tip.

"I gave her five dollars already," I say. "Can you put that on the bill?"

The woman frowns but types something into her computer and then prints out another receipt.

I leave and walk to the bus stop.

Along the way, I stop at a convenience store and buy five dollars' worth of hot dogs and candy. Two hot dogs, with cheese, and three candy bars, on sale. Bright orange stickers below the candy saying SPECIAL! VALUE! I eat everything before the bus comes, even the candy bars, their chocolate gone old, spiderwebbed with gray, and throw all the wrappers away.

Here's a tip: leave no evidence behind.

15

ONCE UPON A TIME, A LITTLE GIRL who lived at 623 Daisy Lane disappeared. The police questioned everyone, even a woman who remembered talking to a man whose little boy had already gone out into the parking lot. She remembered because he asked where the gift shop was and said thank you after she told him.

"No one says thank you anymore," she told the police. "No one's ever grateful for anything."

Ray let me watch her say that on TV, and then turned it off and smiled at me.

16

I GET HOME AT FIVE, WHICH IS AFTER Ray gets home. He works 7–4 every day, with an hour for lunch, loading trucks at a warehouse that ships boxes of ready-to-assemble furniture, the kind that comes with picture instructions and lots of little screws. All our furniture is from there, and all of it leans to one side, manufacturer seconds.

Errors.

My hands are shaking as I close the door behind me.

"What happened?" Ray says. He's still eating his apple. Crunch, crunch, crunch.

"Bus broke down. We had to wait." I sit down at the kitchen table to be judged.

"What bus?"

"75."

He calls the bus company. I watch him throw his apple away. There is still some flesh left, white around the tiny core. I am too nervous to imagine eating it. Also, for once, I am not hungry.

I have not brushed my teeth. I will smell like food.

And Ray will smell it on me.

I look at the knife on the kitchen counter and picture it in my chest. I don't think it would take long for my heart to stop beating.

"All right, thank you," Ray says, and hangs up the phone. He looks at me. "I'm glad you didn't lie to me about the bus, Alice."

I nod. Look right at him.

Does he know about the food?

"Do you have a receipt?"

I fish it out of my pocket and hand it to him. He looks at it, and then throws it in the trash. "Hungry?"

I nod.

Does he know about the food?

He opens the refrigerator. It is the loudest thing in our apartment, makes odd wheezing noises, like it is struggling to stay cold. "You know what will happen if you ever do lie to me, don't you?"

"Yes."

"Good," he says, and slides me a fun-sized container of yogurt. The top promises it's the perfect lunch for children. "Because I would hate to take time off work to drive all the way to 623 Daisy Lane and wait for everyone to come home and . . . take care of things. Helen and Glenn both have new jobs. Did you know that? Do you want to know where they work?"

I shake my head. I open my yogurt. Ray doesn't give me a spoon so I scoop some out with my fingers. My breath will smell okay now.

"I'd hate for them to come home and find me there, waiting for them," he says. "I'd hate for your parents to die because of you."

"I didn't lie to you about the bus," I say.

"I know, silly girl. My girl," he says, and stands up, unbuckles his belt. Opens his pants. "Come over here. Give me a kiss hello."

I get up and walk over to him. He frowns and I hunch over so I barely come up to his shoulder.

"Alice, my baby," he says, kissing my cheek.

Then he shoves me to my knees.

When he's finished, he throws the rest of my yogurt away.

"It spoils so easily," he says. "I wouldn't want you to get sick. Let's go watch TV."

We do. He drinks beer and orders a pizza and puts me

on his lap during the sitcom he hates. I am hungry again now, think of food; hot dogs, candy bars, the pizza crusts inside the box on the floor.

Ray likes how smooth I am, how raw my skin is. It burns by the time he's done touching it.

"No breakfast tomorrow," he says afterward. "I think you might be over 100 pounds. That's not acceptable."

At bedtime, he rumples his sheets—we have a two-bedroom apartment, because we are father and daughter and he wants to take care of me, wants me to have my own room like other little girls—and then crawls into my tiny bed with me. My sheets have pictures of cartoon princesses on them, with pink trim and a matching pink comforter.

"Love you," he says before he falls asleep. I am so hungry my head hurts with it, making me slow, and he pinches my thigh, hard.

"Love you too," I say, but it is too late and he holds me down, breathing hard and fast.

"Show me," he says. "Show me."

So I do.

17

RAY GETS UP AT 6, SHOWERS AND dresses. He whistles while he shaves, and I listen for the clanking hum of the refrigerator, count out its wheezing rhythm. 1, 2, 3 . . . . . . 4. 1, 2, 3 . . . . . . 4.

Ray tried to teach me how to whistle once, in one of his better moods, but I could never pick it up. He said he still loved me anyway.

Lucky me.

"No breakfast, remember?" he says, sitting down next to me on the bed, one paternal hand on my forehead while the other gropes below. He keeps it up until he starts to sweat, little beads of moisture gathering at his temples, and then gets up.

Every Sunday we go to Freedom Church. Ray believes in God, and in looking at all the little girls in their Sunday best, ribbons and bows and tiny socks with lace on them.

The day I got too tall to wear the white dress with short, puffy sleeves and little tucks along the chest, he filled the kitchen sink with water and shoved my head into it.

I was thirteen then, and when I tried to stay down after he'd held me there, lungs burning, inside of my head going dark, he hauled me out and slapped me so hard the right side of my face grew a hand-shaped bruise, jaw to forehead. I couldn't go outside for a week.

No one missed me.

Two days later, when my face was still swollen hot, he came home with a lock of my mother's hair. He wouldn't tell me how he got it, even when I cried and crawled onto his lap to beg the way he likes best.

He just said, "I decide everything. Remember that."

God and monster all in one, and mine to worship.

I tell him to have a good day before he leaves my room, and he turns back to grin, proud.

"I look good today, don't I?"

I nod. He looks like Ray. There are no words for what he looks like to me.

He whistles again as he leaves.

I close my eyes.

There are several women at Freedom Church who

think Ray is attractive, with his full head of hair and carefully pressed clothes. They like that he is so strict with me, they say when they talk to him, his hand resting on my shoulder (remember what I will do if you ever try to leave me, remember who you belong to). Their eyes gleam with hope. They want to be taken care of, and they think Ray could do that for them.

He laughs at them on the way home, laughs at how old and sad they are. "Not like me," he says, and then rests one hand on my knee. "Not like you."

18

EVENTUALLY I GET OUT OF BED AND walk to the bathroom. We don't have a tub, just a shower, but I ignore it and brush my teeth, swallowing the toothpaste instead of spitting it out. I hear it can be poisonous, but I guess it's only if you're really young.

I am 15 now, and I keep waiting for Ray to tire of me. I am no longer short with dimpled knees and frightened eyes. I am almost as tall as he is, and his license says he is 5'7". He likes the picture. He says no one ever takes a good driver's license picture except him.

I am 15 and stretched out, no more than 100 pounds. I can never weigh more than that. It keeps my breasts tiny, my hips narrow, my thighs the size Ray likes.

I am 15 and worn out, tired of everything.

I am 15, and I figure soon he will let me go.

19

THERE WAS ANOTHER ALICE BEFORE me. Ray let her go when she turned 15.

He drove her all the way back to where she used to live, to where she was when she was another girl, back to her before.

Her body was found in a river, floating downstream just a mile from the house she grew up in.

Ray used to tell me this story a lot, pulling me close and saying, "But I'll make sure that doesn't happen to you. I'll keep you safe. All you have to do is be good. Be my little girl forever. You can do that, can't you?"

I am 15, and I figure soon Ray will kill me.

I could run, but he would find me. He would take me

back to 623 Daisy Lane and make everyone who lives there pay.

He would make everyone there pay even if he didn't find me. I belong to him. I'm his little girl.

All I have to do is be good.

20

THIS IS MY DAY:

After I chew on some toothpaste, I go into the living room and turn on the television. Morning television is boring, all bad news and infomercials, but at nine the talk shows start. I lie on the sofa and look at the ceiling.

Sometimes, in the afternoon, if the soaps aren't any good, I'll watch movies about angry, scared women who fight back or teenage girls who suffer but then overcome. There are always shower scenes in them, shots of the women scrubbing their abuse or grief away.

I don't understand this. You can't make yourself clean like that, and fresh-scrubbed skin only invites attention.

Ray makes me shower once a week, and I hate coming out of the bathroom. I hate knowing he's waiting for me, that he will rub his hands and himself all over me and whisper things. His hands used to make me cry, but now I'm used to them.

The thing is, you can get used to anything. You think you can't, you want to die, but you don't. You won't. You just are.

Today I smell like Ray, which is normal, and a little like yesterday's wax. My head itches, and I scratch it until the undersides of my fingernails are bright red. I flick the blood and dead bits of my head onto the floor, and get up to take my pills.

Ray doesn't want me getting pimples or my period, and so he makes me take a pill for both every day. The one for pimples dries out my skin, and makes the sun blotch me angry red. The one to prevent my period does just that, and although the ads on TV say it just makes your period less painful, I never get mine.

I don't ask Ray why.

I only got my period once, late last year, and Ray got so angry he took out a knife and made me sit on a chair in the corner of the living room. He looked at me for a long, long time, and then tied me to the chair and left me there until the bleeding stopped. He wouldn't talk to me, wouldn't look at me. Food and water once a day, a trip to the bathroom each morning and night. One time, I stood up and blood dripped down my leg and onto the carpet and he threw up.

And then he rubbed my face in it.

When the bleeding stopped he made me scrub myself, the chair, the carpet all around it, and then he threw the chair out and gave me the pills.

"We can work this out," he'd said, and cradled me in his arms, my legs cramping from being curled up so I'd fit on his lap. "You're my Alice. You're my little girl. You're all I'll ever want."

21

RAY MET THE ALICE BEFORE ME WHEN he was nineteen and she was eight. He keeps the newspaper clippings from when the police found her body, from the funeral and afterward. Sometimes when he reads them he touches the picture of her in the article, black and white photo of a little lost girl, and cries.

He cries and says he's sorry, so sorry, and do I forgive him? Head on my lap, breath hot on my thighs.

I say yes for her. I say yes and used to figure out how many days until I was fifteen while he hunched over me.

Now it's here, all those days have passed, and I can't help but wonder what he's waiting for.

22

TODAY IS A GOOD DAY ON THE TALK
shows, and I sit and watch people cry and fight
over who fathered their baby and why they love
their cousin and how their moms dress like whores.
The audience is always so excited, so happy with all the
misery.

Sometimes the shows will have on older women with
lost eyes and round faces who cry about being abused
when they were younger. They call their Rays names and
scream, and the host pats their shoulders or gives them
a fast one-armed hug and says things like, "But you sur-
vived. You're strong." Then they will ask why they didn't
say anything.

Why didn't you tell someone?

Why didn't you ask for help?

Why didn't you leave him?

Why didn't you respect yourself enough to get away?

The women usually crumple, shed their flesh shells, and become quivering living dead girls, trapped. A few will say that no one listens, that people don't want to see, and that if you try something, anything, you won't suffer but others will.

The audience always boos and says You Should Have Done Something. You should have fought back. You should have known no one has that kind of power. You should have been strong.

You shouldn't have been so stupid.

The women nod and sniffle. They are still broken. They still agree with everything anyone wants. Even the ones who try to explain end up with their heads down, their hands in their laps. Little girl ready to say she's sorry.

All our fault, always.

23

T HE THING IS, YOU CAN HAVE THAT
kind of power, and everyone in those audiences
knows it. That's why they yell. That's why they
say You Should Have Done Something.

They have power too.

I'd like to see them with it taken away. I'd like to see
What They'd Do then.

24

THE MORE BORING TALK SHOWS, THE ones with celebrities with shiny teeth and musicians who swear their songs are from the heart, are on next. I look out the window at the empty parking lot. Everyone who lives in Shady Pines Apartments works. Everyone has a busy job, long days, and comes home tired. In the five years I've been here, three people have learned my name, and two of them were younger, softer versions of Ray, eggs that hadn't yet rotted. They both told me I could come over "to visit" anytime I wanted.

The third was a woman. She was old, bent and wrinkly, and walked with a cane. She said I should be in school and asked what I was studying when I said my father taught me at home. She sometimes pooped herself and had a daughter, worried-looking and angry, come and take her away three months after she moved in.

The old woman told Ray he was an abomination as she left, but then she also said that to the mailman and the three little boys playing on the sidewalk. Her apartment was rented by the Indian family, a man, a woman, and four little girls. I thought Ray might like the girls but he said they were ugly dark and had bad teeth.

I see them in the hall sometimes, and they never look at me. I am smelly and strange, a dirty-haired girl who doesn't go to school and steals food people leave half-eaten on the washing machines in the basement.

They know I am wrong, and stay away.

I am allowed to eat lunch and I eat yogurt during a soap opera, licking the spoon slowly and carefully, tiny mouthfuls as Storm worries she's in love and Dessen breaks glasses because Emily broke his heart and ran off with his brother and wise Aunt Marge pats worried Henna's hands and tells her that Craig will see that he loves her, that he just needs time. Craig was with Emily before, but now he loves Henna and I think next he will love Susan. She's only a little girl now, but in six months she will be twenty and a doctor or a lawyer and will swear she hates him right before she kisses him.

I love soap operas. If I lived in a town like Ridgefield,

Aunt Marge would see me and invite me in and then call her daughter or son, who would be a cop or a lawyer, and they would come and rescue me and I'd live with them, and their children wouldn't like me but would come to love me after I saved them from almost drowning or burning to death. I would never have to eat or even be hungry.

I would always be listened to.

25

WHEN RAY COMES HOME AT 4:30, I pour him a glass of milk. He doesn't believe in drinking alcohol; his mother told him it was a sin. I rub his back and feet while he watches the judge shows that come on before the news.

He likes Judge Hammer, who was a military judge and who yells, "Justice hurts!" when people cry during his verdicts. Today's case is about a man who says his ex-girlfriend owes him money and took his car. Hammer tells the ex-girlfriend, who is chewing gum and leaning forward so the camera can see down her shirt, to pay up, and Ray says, "What a crock. Anyone can tell that guy is lying."

I nod—Ray thinks children should be seen and not heard, just like his mother taught him—and he sighs, scratches his stomach, and continues. "Did you see how he kept blinking? Classic sign. You know, I went to Alice's funeral and talked to her parents and said I wished I knew why she'd run away all those years ago, and they had no idea she was with me because I knew not to blink like that. They had no idea how much she loved me." He sighs. "How much I loved her."

He strokes my hair. "She was never as good as you."

I press my hands to Ray's feet, stare at the yellow undersides of his socks. I've seen enough television to know Ray is missing something other than his soul. It's like you see him, and he's a person, but if you look close enough, you can tell that he's not. Like underneath his skin, he's not hollow. He's rotted out.

"You're too tall, though," he says, frowning, and pushes my hands off his feet, dragging me up toward him. Hands on my throat. "Too tall and you want to leave me, don't you? You'd run away in a second if I let you. You wouldn't care if everyone at 623 Daisy Lane had to die for you. So selfish."

"I don't want to leave," I tell him, cracking out the words as the world goes fuzzy around the edges. "I want to stay with you."

"Liar." He squeezes harder. "You always say that, and then one day I'll come home and have to track you down,

find you talking to people, maybe telling them stories."
He frowns. "My mother hated storytelling. You know
what she used to do to me when I did it?"

I can't breathe, but that's not why he lets the pressure
up. He lets go a little so I can nod. Because he knows I
will. I am not strong; I cannot stop him or even slow him
down. I can only wait until he gets so tired of me that he
lets me die and moves on.

"She would punish me," he says. "Hold me down and
show me how all we think of is sin. How we are all sin."
He spits the last word out, like he can taste it, and then
touches my hair, slides his fists under my shirt and twists
the sullen rise of my right breast, the little lump that's
there. "Would you be that kind of mother?"

"No."

Ray has never come out and said it, but I know from
years of listening to him dream that his mother did to him
what he does to me. Held him down, rubbed him raw,
broke him open. In them, he cries and begs her not to
touch him, that he doesn't want to go inside her, that he is
a good boy, he really is.

I let Ray have his nightmares, watch him thrash and
listen to his voice squeak with fear. I lie there and watch
him and wish he was trapped back there, with her, and
had never broken free.

But his mother died when he was eighteen, burned

47

to death because she fell asleep smoking a cigarette. Ray got an insurance check from the church school where she worked as a secretary and moved away.

He met the first Alice a year later.

His mother never smoked. But she was such a private woman, he's told me, that people just assumed she'd kept it a secret. She seemed the type to do that.

"You aren't listening," Ray says, and his hands tighten again. "You know you're supposed to listen when I talk." He shoves me to the floor and pulls off my pants.

I stare at the ceiling while he sweats and thrusts, air aching down my throat and into my lungs until he grabs my hair and says, "I know what I'm going to do. What's going to change."

He pushes faster then, harder, and slams my head into the floor over and over until my vision is bright and fuzzy and there are strands of my hair caught in his hand.

I think of the knife in the kitchen, of the bridges I've seen from the bus or on the way to church or the super-market (Ray and I go every Saturday morning. Ray stares at little girls and I stare at the food), and feel my heart cramp.

It will be over soon, finally, but the thing about hearts is that they always want to keep beating.

They want to keep beating, and when Ray's finished he says, "I like that. A family. You'd be a good mother, wouldn't you? Let me watch out for a little girl of our own? Let me take care of her? Help me teach her everything she needs to know?"

"A little girl?" In all the dreams I have had, and they are small dreams, bloody ones that end with me floating free, I never dreamed this.

He shivers into me, grinning sharper. "She'll be so bad at first, crying and whining and maybe even screaming." He fingers my hair. "You cried, remember? You screamed. And now look at you. Happy as can be."

I nod, mind as numb as the rest of me. He is not letting me go. He wants me to stay. He wants me to find a girl for him.

For us.

He can't mean it. I will find him one, a beautiful little stupid girl, as dumb as the one at 623 Daisy Lane used to be, and show her to him. He will want her, with her little limbs and happy face and solid, live flesh.

She will become the new Alice, and he will want her so much he will forget all about me. Kill me to teach her a lesson, probably, and then move on. Yes, that is what will happen.

What must happen.

"I'll help you," I tell him. "I'll find what you need."

He kisses my cheek and then rolls off me, motioning for me to get up. "That's my girl."

Not for much longer, I think, and bend over, touch my fingers to my curled up mouth.

"I see that," Ray says, and yanks my jaw up, looks at me. "I see that smile. You want to help me, don't you? You want to teach our girl everything I like."

I nod, and he shoves me down again, forgetting dinner in his visions of this girl to come, this new child. This new me.

26

I AM ALLOWED TO LEAVE THE HOUSE the next afternoon.

Ray has given me bus fare and told me the name of a park he wants me to go see. It is close to the apartment but not too close, a short ride in his truck but a long ride on the bus, and he tells me to remember everything I see.

I get to the park after sitting on two buses, and blink at all the people there. So many of them, and all so young. I will never remember everything but find a bench that has bags and backpacks tossed in a stack near it anyway, watch kids run over and pull out snacks and drinks, trailing crumbs everywhere.

I try to focus, but the world is dizzy, spinning as I

think of what I will find here. Ray's prize. The new me.

She has to be just right. She has to make him forget everything.

Or at least me.

I take a breath, to slow the world down, and look.

I look and see a girl there. And there. And over there. I grab a notebook, pick up a pencil.

The first girl is blond and a little chubby, a thumb sucker. Ray would like teaching her not to do that. I carefully write down blonde and thumb.

She has a babysitter or mother, though, a woman who brings her a foil-wrapped package that the girl bats away, annoyed. Ray won't like the mother/babysitter hovering around. But still. People can be distracted, and Ray really doesn't like wasting food.

The other girls I see are both dark-haired like me, and both are alone, maybe dropped off by an older brother or sister who has to "watch" them, or maybe they've sworn to go straight home after school but come here instead. They don't play so much as stand, sullen, watching the others. They would scream and kick, I can tell. Ray would like that too. I write scream and kick, 2, and then sit with my face turned toward the sun. I don't bother to close my eyes.

"Have you seen my notebook?"

I blink, light burning away, and see a girl standing

in front of me. Six? Seven? Eight? Doesn't matter. She's young.

She's young, brownish-blond hair, and is ferociously clean and shiny, not a speck of dirt on her little white shirt or pink skirt with a smiling flower on the hem.

"Notebook?"

"It's green and has a frog on it," she says. "I went on the swings and now it's not here."

"It's not," I say, and stroke my fingers over the cover of the notebook I am holding closed against my chest. Tracing over the big frog sticker. "Someone must have taken it."

"And my pencil."

"And your pencil."

She sighs and sits down. "It's my favorite. My dad gave it to me for my birthday."

"Oh," I say, and snap the pencil in half, grinning as its pieces fall to the ground under the bench we are sitting on.

"I don't like you," she says abruptly. "You're not nice."

She gets up and goes over to the swings. I lean over and pick up half the pencil from under the bench. I write ALICE in large letters on the page, then tear it out and leave the notebook on the bench, half the broken pencil beside it.

I have found Ray's new girl. I have found the new me.

I think about her all the way home, how she will cry and scream and plead just like I did.

It makes me smile.

Everyone on the bus who sees me smile looks away. They see that I am all wrong, that my smile means someone else's pain.

But no one says anything.

27

THREE LIFE LESSONS:

1. No one will see you.
2. No one will say anything.
3. No one will save you.

I know what the once upon a time stories say, but they lie.

That's what stories are, you know. Lies.

Look at that, four life lessons. Now you owe me.

28

AT HOME, RAY IS TIRED AND CRANKY and makes me step on the scale three times before I'm allowed dinner. I give him what I wrote, the page marked ALICE, before he gives me my yogurt, and for a moment I think he's going to take it away but he doesn't.

"You can't write worth shit," is all he says. "Good thing you got me around to take care of you."

I swallow a spoonful of yogurt and ask to get a glass of water. Ray won't let me get it, but instead brings it to me, motioning for me to get up so he can sit in my chair.

"Tell me about them," he says, throwing the paper away

and patting his lap for me to sit back down, to curl into him, and I do.

His hands are gripping my arms hard before I've even finished describing the first one, and I don't get to finish my yogurt. Later, he lets me eat the burned bit of his TV dinner meatloaf while he watches two doctors argue over how to treat a dying boy.

"Tell me about them again," he says when all the lights are out except for the fairy princess night light he's plugged into my bedroom wall, waving her magic wand to spread pink light into the room.

I imagine her melting, real light coming out of her, flame bright. Ray lying snoring as she burns, waking up when it's far too late. That would be a real fairy godmother thing to do.

"Pretty," I tell Ray. "They were pretty."

"What were they wearing?"

I make up outfits, frilly little dresses with sashes and tiny white socks folded into delicate shoes. That was how he dressed me for years, until the dresses strained open across my hips and chest, until my arms came out strangled red from the binding sleeves.

"I wish we could have them all," he says. "But we can't be greedy. Being greedy is bad. Like you tonight, eating that meat. Did you think I wouldn't see you?"

"I—" I say and then stop, still, made stupid by telling

stories about those girls, forgetting that none of them are here, that there's still only one he can wrap his claws around.

"You can make it up to me," he whispers, a ghost that is all too real in my ear. Hot hands squeezing me too tight, but only where people won't see.

And even if he decorated my neck with a ring of finger-prints and left me lying in the street, no one would notice. Not in Shady Pines, where everyone is busy working to keep their kids fed, their bills barely paid. Not anywhere, because I am nothing, unseen.

I learned that the hard way.

29

I DON'T REMEMBER MY FIRST WEEK WITH
Ray, those days when I was being made into Alice,
except for one thing. One thing that showed me
everything he said was true, that no one wanted me back,
that I had to stay with him, that if I didn't listen bad
things would happen.

I woke up at some point, broken and bruised, Ray
asleep snoring on top of me. I wiggled like a fish and
slipped out from under him, throwing on a neat pile of
clothes lying on a table. Little-girl-who-had-cream-soda-
lip-gloss clothes. Little-girl-who-knew-she-couldn't-go-
outside-undressed clothes.

Normal little girl clothes.

There was one door in the room and I opened it, stepped out into a parking lot lit by a flickering, dying streetlight, a small faded sign by the road reading ROUTE 40 MOTEL—WEEKLY RATES AVAILABLE.

Across the street was a gas station, the kind with a store that sold food and had people.

I didn't wait to cross. I ran. I ran as fast as I could, ran straight for the signs advertising SODA: 2 FOR $2! And HOTDOGS: NOW WITH FREE TOPPINGS!

There were no cars, but inside a woman sat behind a big sheet of plastic, chewing gum and watching TV. She had dark hair, like my mother, and as soon as I saw her I started to cry.

She looked up, and I waited for her to get up. To come and save me. But all she said was, "We don't allow no one in here without shoes, even kids. You over at pump eight?"

"Sure am," Ray said, and clamped one hand around my arm. I cried harder, words finally starting to come, rising up as I realized I had to get her to listen, to see what was really happening.

And then Ray leaned over and whispered, "Shut up or I'll drive back to your house, not to take you home but to kill your parents and make you watch. Make you see what happens to little girls who don't listen."

I didn't want my parents to die, and I already knew Ray

would do it. That he would and could and did lie about other things—Don't move and I won't hurt you. Tell me where you live and I swear I'll take you home now. Being good is fun, and you want to be good, don't you?—but he wasn't lying about this.

He took me to his car. He had a car then, a white one with a narrow backseat that I can still see even with my eyes wide open, and to this day TV where people twist around each other in cars makes something inside me scream and I have to change the channel or stay very still and not let Ray see that I hurt because my pain makes him want to hold me. Hurt me more.

I sat in the car and he paid for gas and we drove away and he pulled over onto a long wooded road and raised his fists, then pain inside and out blurring everything, breaking everything.

After that, I was Alice.

I am Alice, and Ray dreams in the night, happy dreams that wake him up and make him roll me over, my head pressed into the pillow. Suffocation looks so easy but no matter how hard I press my face down, no matter how I try to breathe in fabric, not air, there is no escape for me.

He sleeps with one arm thrown across me after, and I lie stinging sharp all over, a wet sticky puddle under me. Soon there will be a little girl here, a real one with tiny arms and legs for Ray to push into.

I want him to take her tomorrow. I want that little girl here now, where I am. I want her to be Ray's love, to bear it. I don't care that TV and the preacher at church say that children are treasures or little miracles or special.

They are flesh and blood like the shell around me, a thing waiting to be molded by someone's will, and Ray wants that job. I don't care if he takes it. If he takes everyone and everything, every child from every place. I just want him to leave me.

30

MORNING SAME AS ALWAYS, MY shows, my wait for food, except I have to wash my sheets, bleach in the washer to get out the stains. There is no one around so I pour bleach right onto the spot, watch the yellow and brown-red stain ooze, let the sharp burning smell of the bleach cramp the inside of my head.

I clean too, because Ray likes a clean house, dusting and vacuuming and picking up the socks he leaves around the apartment like little smelly snakes, curling them into his laundry basket. I get tired during, the room spinning around and around, and lie on the floor listening to the refrigerator and my heart beating loud and fast, thumpthumpthump in my chest.

Eat my yogurt, sour taste on my tongue, container warm in my hand. The refrigerator is angry with me too. I go get the sheets out of the dryer and steal four quarters someone has left on top of the washing machine.

There is a vending machine in the building but I don't use it. What if someone saw me eating and told Ray? He says hello to the people around us, casual waves and occasional chats about the weather. I am shy, so I only say hello, pain if I don't say it the way Ray wants or if he just feels like it.

"Homeschooling must be tough for you, what with you working and all," someone once said to him, a brassy-haired lady with three little boys and a round pregnant stomach. "God bless you for being so devoted to your child. I'm going to do the same for mine, once Devon gets that promotion and I don't have to wait tables no more."

Devon ran off, and after a while, she got evicted. Before that, her little boys often had split lips and black and blue stained legs, and they stayed home from school, playing in the laundry room, more than they ever went. No one ever said a word to her either. I used to twist the tender skin at the back of their necks until they'd go into their apartment and bring me cookies. I could tell from looking at them that they'd never say a word to anyone.

I was sorry when they left, even though I'd stopped making them bring me cookies when I saw them flinch as I came into the laundry room one day. Ray fed me more often then, though. Now I think they could flinch all they wanted and I'd hurt them until my belly was full.

I stop at a gas station on the way to the park, peanut butter crackers paid for and stuffed in my mouth, one two three four five six. The woman behind the counter had dark hair but no one reminds me of my mother anymore.

The park is very crowded, older kids talking and smoking, the ones that don't fit in taking time to push the smaller ones around, laughing at their power and how it works. The two dark-haired little girls from yesterday turn out to be biters, scrappy little things with snapping teeth, and when an older man, harmless because his eyes are nothing like Ray's, asks them if they need help they scream and scream until a policewoman wanders over and asks what's going on, looking bored and rubbing the small of her back.

I will have to tell Ray there are cops around. He will not like that. He will not like the two little girls anymore, either. They have seen things, I can tell from their screams, and they will spot him right away. They both look at me when they leave, dragged out by an older boy with fuzz above his upper lip and dirt under his fingernails.

No, they will not do. They are rattling hollow under their scowling eyes, life being drained out of them already. Ray will not want that. He will want someone whose eyes need to be opened.

I look for the little blond girl, the thumb sucker, but she is not there. I only see notebook girl, the bossy thing who actually spoke to me. She is sitting on the swings, eyes vacant as she looks up into the sky. I can't figure out what she's doing. She doesn't look like she's trying to think out of something, but like she's trying to think into it.

"She's pretending she's a cloud."

I look and see a boy watching me. His eyes are like Ray's, hungry, but it's a simple hunger, easy to read. He is looking at me like how boys look at the girls who live below us when they talk to them on the stairs, hands under their shirts as the girls giggle and then pretend they want to stop when they see me.

"I just came to get her and bring her home," he says, sitting down next to me, thigh pushing against mine. He is skinny, with long bony fingers. "You go to school around here?"

"No," I say, and since I haven't moved my leg away, he leans in toward me. His breath smells like pizza. Ray used to let me eat pizza. I remember the taste of cheese, of pepperoni, grease on my lips.

"Want to hang out?" he says, and I notice that behind

the hunger his eyes are dazed, like he doesn't or can't or won't see the world. "My car is right behind us, and I've got some pills . . ."

"What's your sister's name?"

He blinks at me. "Lucy. I'm Jake. Guess I should have said that before."

I shrug. He grins, nervous. See his gums, they are pink-red, shiny. "So, you wanna . . . ?"

I nod.

He takes my hand, walks me to his car. Long walk, car in the back of the parking lot, shadowed by trees. All alone. Hiding place. There is a piece of sidewalk, broken, right beside it.

There has been one other boy. It was when I was fourteen, right after Ray put me on the pill. He whistled at me when I walked to the bathroom at the back of the supermarket, Ray telling me to hurry up while he waited in line at the pharmacy counter for his cholesterol pills.

The whistling boy came up to me by the bathroom and asked if I wanted company. He had bright red pimples, angry oozing sores, all over his face, and when I said yes he blinked and turned like he was going to run away until I dropped to my knees in front of him.

I did it because he was so surprised-looking and because his skin was so angry-looking and because I saw he saw my eyes and thought about running. I did it because he was nothing. I did it because I wished Ray had used the knife instead of tying me to a chair.

Ray saw my mouth when I came back and knew. I couldn't sit down for a week afterward, and my back, from my shoulders to about my knees, was purple black, then yellow green, for ages. Both my little fingers have crooked knuckles now, and ache before it rains.

Jake's car is expensive, smell of money underneath the ripe scent of boy. I do not take the pills Jake offers, I know nothing can take away the world. I just push him down into his seat and open his zipper.

"The backseat's wider," he says, but I shake my head and when he tries to threaten, his hands grabbing my hair, I dig my fingers into them, right into his skin, until he moves them away.

When I'm done, I sit up and wipe my mouth with the back of my hand. He is looking at me, glassy-eyed still, but something in my face changes that, makes his expression shift, go alarmed. Almost frightened.

"You . . ." he says, trailing off, and I realize what he sees. That this was nothing to me, that his want was not mine. Is not mine.

I lean in, staring at his eyes more closely. His face turns red.

"I have to go," he says. "Get—get out of the car." Mouth works, and he spits out, "bitch," but it's a whimper. I smile to let him know I know his word is nothing, and he shivers, glassy eyes blinking fast.

I watch him go, then circle around and stand by a cluster of trees almost out of sight of the swings. Lucy is still staring at the clouds. Still dreaming.

Jake comes back for her later, face smoothed out, the pills I saw him take swimming through him. He tells Lucy something, and she stops swinging but doesn't come with him. She is still watching the sky. I wait for him to grab her arm, but he doesn't. He just waits, hands shoved in his pockets, shoulders hunched, and eventually she looks away from the clouds and walks, turning in wide circles and telling stories, out of the park.

I walk to the bus stop and wait. On the way back, I try to picture having things I want, like mountains of food or sleeping without Ray beside me, but I can't. I can only see Ray's face when I tell him there is a girl and that I know how we can get her. I can only see his reaction when I tell him my plan.

I can't dream of clouds, but I can see the knife on the kitchen counter. I can dream of it inside me, opening me up and closing me down.

31

RAY IS WAITING WHEN I GET HOME, and one look at my face sends his fist smash crashing into me, CRACK into my chest, right near my heart.

"I can see all the way inside you," he spits, red-faced, voice deadly low. "I see that you don't understand anything. Alice, I expected better from you."

Curled up on the floor, white spots in my vision as I wiggle for air, wheezing in nothing as my body stops working for a moment, stunned, and I don't understand why it starts working again. I don't understand why my shell keeps living. Breathing. Why won't it listen to me, to the little part I have that isn't Ray, to that tiny once upon a time girl who just wants to close her eyes and never wake up again?

623 Daisy Lane. Helen and Glenn.

That's why. Once upon a time, I belonged to them and they shouldn't suffer for that.

Ray sits down next to me on the floor. "I'm tired of this," he says. "I love you, I trust you, I tell you what I want, and what do you do? Hurt me." He bends over and pushes my hair off my forehead, crooked bangs he trimmed for me because Alice has bangs.

Alice has bangs and loves him, loves him.

He puts one hand on my throat, higher up than normal, and the pressure is a sharp hot flare of pain, bright like light, and I am talking, babbling, grinding out words through a cracked throat I have a plan never hurt you never leave you love you please love you please.

I am the living dead girl because I am too weak to die. I hate those crying dough women on TV because they are just like me, weak and broken and clinging to the hands that hold us under.

"Plan?" Ray says, still red-faced, spit flecking his mouth, this was what the last Alice saw maybe, the Alice who wasn't as afraid as I am. Who was so much stronger.

I dream of a knife in my chest but will never plunge it in. Will beg and plead to keep it away when Ray pushes it into me.

I strangle out my plan in broken words as Ray puts ice on my throat and rubs my ribs and carries me to the sofa, careful tender as he opens my clothes and marks me all over.

"This boy comes and picks up his sister," he says, rubbing my feet while he stares at the dark TV. Turned off and silent, he still stares at it, playing out stories in his head.

"But not until she's been there awhile," I say, my toes curling up under his fingers, my throat hot with pain. I touch one hand to the fist-shaped bruise blooming near my heart. At least my feet don't hurt. Ray knows how to rub feet. He used to do it a lot for his mother, back when he was young.

"What does his car look like?"

"Red," I say, and when Ray pauses, hands hovering over my feet, I spit out what I can remember.

He starts rubbing my feet again, nodding. "So I get her, and when the boy comes, you keep him busy—I know you can do that (eyes going angry, and bitter pressure on my feet)—and then I'll come find you, take care of him, and we'll—" He pauses, eyes gleaming, and his fingers skate feather light over my feet. "We'll put Annabel's things in his car, a little dirt and blood on them. Maybe a little on him. And then we vanish and he's left with a story of a girl who can't be found." He chuckles. "Two, even."

Annabel. He is not calling her Alice. My bruised heart flutters, a trapped bird. "Annabel?"

"We'll go to the desert," he says. "I decided that today. The desert for sure. You, me, and baby girl makes three. At night you'll sit and hold her hands while I show her how lucky she is to be loved."

He is breathing faster now and pulls me toward him, a yank on my ankles drawing my rag-doll body in, lower half pushed against him.

"You'll hold her," he says, and everything I own is easily pushed down, away, clothes falling off me like water. "You'll hold her and I'll love her."

He grins at me. "You'll like that, won't you?"

I nod because he wants me to. I nod because I will. She will get his love and I will hold her down to take it all because then there will be none for me.

I cannot save myself, and I do not want to save her.

32

THE ALICE BEFORE ME, HER PARENTS were named Bob and Megan. They cried so much at her funeral, at her coming home, that Ray says it's a wonder they lived long enough to ever see her come home at all.

These are the kind of stories Ray tells.

His stories are always true, which doesn't make them stories at all.

33

I N THE MORNING, RAY MAKES ME GET
up when he does, puts me in the shower and hums
as he lathers soap and rubs his hands across me.

I sit naked and cold on the bed while he opens the
safe he keeps in his room, all his paychecks cashed and
stored in a fireproof, destruction-proof box with a com-
bination only he knows. He pays for everything in cash,
no checks or credit cards like his mother always used,
spending money she didn't have and then blaming him
when everything got taken away.

He counts the money once, twice, numbers falling from
his lips like a song, and he's humming again when he's
done.

"We'll be able to go somewhere nice," he says. "Maybe someplace with a pool. I'll watch Annabel swim. A little blue suit with yellow trim for her, and you'll dry her off with a towel, then wrap her up and bring her to me."

I will do that, will unroll her from the towel and make it so she's wearing only her shriveled, clammy skin, and leave her to Ray. I will steal her food to keep her tiny, to keep him happy. I will put her on his knee at night and let her hear his bedtime stories.

"We'll need sunscreen," I say. "So she doesn't burn."

He nods, pleased, and then picks out what I must wear. Not my black pants that sag around my waist and hips, that droop over my feet, that I wear every day. Not my gray T-shirt, his until he got tomato sauce on the hem, tiny holes on the sleeves from my fingers picking at the fabric while the day passes.

I have to wear jeans, dark and stiff and too small, cutting into my waist and leaving my ankles bare. My shirt is pink, pale like the first blush of hurt skin, just a little blow to let you know you are here, that you are not leaving. That you must open your eyes and see.

Pink like Ray makes me. I know that and he does too because he smiles big and fond and rubs the bruise on my chest, saying, "Remember? Remember how you used to be?"

I remember.

After I am dressed, he tells me what I will do. I will get to the park earlier than before, will miss my soap opera to be there on time. I will watch Lucy. I will wait for Jake, talk to him—and Ray narrows his eyes then, mouth biting off the word "talk" as his hands shake me back and forth.

"You do know what that means, right?" he says, and I nod.

I know.

"You get the boy to come tomorrow too," he says. "Then everything can happen. Tomorrow morning we'll pack up, spend the day together, and then I'll pick up Annabel and come get you. Leave a present for the boy."

He means it, really means it. I think. "What will we take with us?"

He looks at me, and then a slow grin breaks across his face. His gums are red like meat.

"Everything," he says, and walks into his room, comes back with folded, printed pages.

Newspaper clipping in my hand, tiny girl with a bow in her hair grinning toothlessly. Vanessa Judith, miracle baby, born six months ago to Helen and Glenn. One daughter, gone long ago, and now a new one. Every day I think of what I lost, Helen says. And every day I'm glad God decided to give me a second chance.

We can't go back, we can't forget, Glenn says. But we

want to live each day as it comes. In memory of what we lost, and in honor of what we have.

"Isn't that sweet?" Ray says, and I stare at the baby, so tiny, so new.

"Hey," he says, grabbing my chin, forcing my eyes to meet his. "Mess this up and we'll drive to 623 Daisy Lane and I'll burn everything. Little girl that replaced you. Mommy. Daddy. All gone."

He cups my jaw in his hands. "Mommy and Daddy and I'll hear them screaming and let you hear it too. Then I'll leave you there, roll you in their ashes and put matches in your hands, and when the police come they'll know you were bad and ran away and came back to punish them for forgetting you. After all, you sent those angry letters home. They gave them to the police and hope you never come back."

Letters? I never . . . Ray grins at me. God-monster, ruler of my world.

When I don't say anything, he kisses my forehead. "Be good today. Be very, very good."

He is whistling when he leaves for work.

I stare at the picture of the baby for a long, long time, and then put it back in Ray's room, face up on his dresser, next to his hairbrush and picture of his mother. Her hair was dark too.

34

ONCE UPON A TIME, THERE WAS A
little girl. Now there is a new one.
There is always a new one.

35

MORNING, MY MORNING. I LIE ON the sofa and watch TV. After a while I get up and get the piece of paper I brought home for Ray out of the trash, turning it over to the clean side. I find a pen in the kitchen, next to where he keeps the shopping list, same things on it every week, and sit down at the table.

Dear Vanessa Judith,
You look pretty in the paper, shiny new
not broken. Be better than I was, am.
I didn't write the letters that came. I never
wrote any letters but this one. Don't ever

listen to anyone who asks if you want
to know where I am.

I stop and put the paper in my pocket. It's a stupid letter
and I can't find the words to say what I want, feeling happy
she's here and safe, angry she is so pretty and new and not
smeared like me, and babies can't read anyway. Stupid.

In the park, I crumple it inside my fist, squeezing tight,
and drop it into a trash can.

"You were here yesterday, weren't you?" someone asks,
not Jake, not a boy, but a woman, and I turn to see the
tired-looking cop staring at my hand still crushed into a
fist, red from where I squeezed the paper like I could force
the words out and let them float up into the sky.

Ray does not like cops. Once one came to the door
to ask if we'd seen a guy who'd stolen two cars, and then
asked me if I was sick because he said I looked pale and
Ray said I had the flu and did the officer have a card, he
would call if he heard anything and then sat watching
the door for two hours after the cop left, knife in his
hand with my throat right under it. Waiting.

I don't like cops either.

"I thought you were homeless yesterday," the cop says.
"The clothes and everything. But then how do I know
how kids dress now? Where do you go to school?" She
squints at me. "What happened to your throat?"

Across from me, a little boy kicks another little boy in the leg.

"Fight," I say. "My brother."

"He do that a lot?"

I shake my head no. She is still looking at me.

"You hungry?"

I shake my head no again but she pulls out a candy bar, and my hands are reaching for it even as she says, "I bought this earlier but it melted some and I hate melted . . . oh. You are hungry."

I do not look at her as I swallow, breaking the candy apart with my teeth, breaking it as fast as I can to get it inside me.

"When's the last time you ate?" she asks.

"Lunch." That is the right answer and I did eat yogurt for the first five minutes of my soap, Storm waiting to see if her baby was all right or if it was going to be born with a rare disease that only the doctor she used to love could cure. Then I had to run for the bus, heart thump-thumpthumping in my chest.

"I'm Barbara," the cop says, holding out her hand, and I think I pause too long before I take it. Her skin is very warm.

"Cold hands you've got there," she says, and pulls something out of her pocket. A card, which she hands to me.

SAFE HARBOR, it says.

"It's a special place," she says. "For teenagers who don't—who might need a safe place."

There are no safe places, but I nod and say thank you like Ray did when he got the card from the police officer and put it in my pocket like I will keep it.

"I have to go now," Barbara says, and touches my arm. I try not to flinch but no one other than Ray and the waxer who rips off flesh and sees my parted legs as money touches me, and I don't like it, I don't like hands on me. I have Ray's and they are so heavy I feel them all the time.

Barbara nods like I have told her a secret and walks off. I wait until she is all the way over in the trees, near the swings where I am supposed to be, and then I turn around and leave.

On the bus, I try to think of how to tell Ray what has happened. How I can say it so he will not think I have taken Annabel away from him and then think about what he said this morning and decide to do it.

There is no way I can say "cop" without him getting angry. I take the card out of my pocket and tear it into tiny pieces that I sprinkle into the bag of the old woman sitting with me, jealously clutching her shopping bags like I want to steal her oranges and grapes.

I do, but I won't.

When I get home Ray is there, sitting on the sofa, waiting, and as soon as I see him I open my mouth and say, "She's sick, so we can't get her tomorrow, but soon."

"Sick?"

I have lied to Ray. I have never lied to Ray, not since the gas station and what happened after, and I know he will know I am lying, but what he does is frown and say, "Did the boy say with what?"

I shake my head.

"Stupid," Ray says, and I start to sink to the floor, ready to crawl and beg, anything, but then he says, "Annabel will thank us for getting her away from people who don't take good care of her, won't she?" His eyes are gleaming and he stands up and he has been thinking about her while I've been gone and then whispers what he will do to her, what I will help him do, while I lie silent under him.

Inside my bruised chest my heart beats a fluttering song, tiny notes but still there because I didn't tell Ray the truth and he believed me.

Make his dinner, the corn gets into the potatoes and I have to apologize for that for a long time. My jaw is tired afterward, aching from being forced open, and my head hurts from where he grabbed it, clutching, and he turns to me when the lights are out and we are tucked into my pink bed, but I listen to my heart singing its tiny song and wonder.

36

THIS IS THE SONG:

>I lied, and he didn't know it.
>I lied, and he didn't know it.
>I lied, and he didn't know it.

Ray doesn't know everything.

37

MORNING AGAIN, ALWAYS MORNING
again, always another day, and I actually eat
breakfast with lunch, one yogurt, two, I
am so lost in dreaming.

I hadn't known I could still do that, thought my head
only painted pictures of things that had blurred around
the edges; those first few weeks with Ray or strange,
faraway glimpses of that once upon a time girl and her
happy, silly, stupid life.

But I am dreaming, and I even have a plan. I know
from talk shows and soap operas, my school, that plans
have to be simple. I can't depend on one moment for
everything, can't expect that Ray won't be thinking

of things I could do and planning ahead himself.

I will get him Annabel. I will go to the park, talk to Jake, and Ray will take her. He will show her what she must do, what happens if you don't listen, don't behave.

Then, when he is ready to go, I'll be gone. I will do more than talk to Jake. I will do whatever he wants and then open the door, piece of broken sidewalk in my hand, crack smack him down to sleep. Lay him out on the ground to dream.

I will take his car. I've never driven before but I've seen Ray do it, seen people on TV do it, and I will get the key. The car will have gas in it, and Jake will have money—he must have money or a credit card, everyone on TV has one—and I will go. Jake on the ground, waiting to be found, bet Ray will find him first.

But I will be gone.

I will be gone, and Ray will have to decide. New Annabel, so smooth and young, with a body that does not have to be tamed into a straight line—or me.

Little baby girl, with so much to learn, or me?

He will pick her, better and newer, and I will drive. I remember 623 Daisy Lane, located in Harbor View. Four hours from here, Ray says, has always said, and I can do that. Go there.

I will go there, tell them they have to leave. That they are not safe. I will see . . . I will see them. I will make sure they are all right and that they go, and they will want . . .

They will not want me with them. I can't even get a blurry picture of that in my head, can't see them reaching toward me when I am covered with Ray, so full of him I'm empty. But they will go and I will . . .

I don't know. Hide, definitely. Burn down 623 Daisy Lane after they leave and wait for the police.

Yes. Ray will not come for me if the police have me. If they have me, he won't be able to get me. I will be in jail. I will stay in until I am old, twenty-five, thirty, eat all I can and hope I swell up, push out into breasts and hips and belly like his mother's wide white girth.

Then, if he comes, he will not want me. I will be safe.

I am usually a husk, rattling through each day, but now I . . . I feel. I feel smart. I feel . . . I feel good. The sensation is strange, tiny stabs of something like pain but not, like . . . like when Ray is tired from work and falls asleep on the sofa and I get to curl into myself for a whole evening.

Those nights, legs arms chest feet thighs and everything over and around and under and between—all mine—those nights almost shine. I feel dizzy at that, the thought of my skin not his but mine, and my body, my hollow shell, directed by my hands. Forever and ever, mine.

My body coming together and taking me away.

I do not care about Storm, even though today is the day she finds out if the doctor she destroyed can save her baby. Ray said I should go to the park and talk to Jake, ask about Annabel, get images to paint him a picture of her flushed skin, her tiny tired legs and arms tucked into bed, little girl needing care.

"Make sure to find out when she'll be back," he said. "Make sure."

I nodded, already knowing what the answer would be, she will be there tomorrow, oh yes, she will, and I get to the park extra early, before any children arrive. Sun on my face and I wiggle my toes back and forth in my shoes, eager.

Yes I worry about what I will say to Jake, has to be words today, has to be, Ray will be watching, but words are just letters, right? A. L. I. C. E. Put them together, pull them apart, make new ones. I can do that, have to do that.

Can do that for legs arms stomach back chest elbows knees of mine to be all mine.

Lucy, now Annabel, comes in, little red backpack. She was going to toss it on the ground, but stops when she sees me.

Look at her. Little girl, Ray will want her, and I will be alone, my skin my own. Thought washing over me again and again, joy.

"You're crying," she says. Not a question, no wondering

why, and I touch my face. It is wet, the skin on my cheeks tightening as it dries. Like it will crack if I open my mouth.

"You don't cry?" I ask her, and my skin stays in place. If she doesn't, Ray will take her and never look back, forget all about me. I didn't cry either. Not until I met him.

She shrugs. "No. Jake says only babies cry and I'm not a baby even though he says I am."

"Babies are little."

She looks at me like I'm stupid. "Right. And I'm not. I can touch the sky when I swing. I can go that high."

I nod. Touch fingers to my face, still wet, so glad it will be her, not me, that I'm overflowing.

"You should stop crying," she says, her little face frowning, and then she pats my knee. Her hands are tiny. "You aren't a baby anymore."

"No," I say, but my voice is a little girl cry, soft and weak. Ray has taught me only one way to speak. "I'm not."

I watch her swing, this little girl who I will help Ray take, who will learn she is a baby, helpless as one and born into a place where she cannot grow, where she must stay as she is now even though her body will try to change.

Ray will hurt her. Pain and tears soothed with ice cream and threats. Maybe she will try to run too, wake up and race for the world only to end up on the side of the road like me, the world turning into a blur that ends only when she wakes up naked and bloody and broken. Reborn.

Better her than me.

"Hello again," Barbara says, leaning into where I'm looking, following my eyes to the little girl on a swing, feet pointed toes-up at the sky. Enjoy it while you can, Annabel. "You know her?"

I shake my head.

"I saw you talking to her. She's good on the swings, isn't she? Are you taking her somewhere later?"

I shake my head no and I am not, not really. Ray will. I will just help.

"You sure?"

"Where would I take her?"

Barbara shrugs. "Just asking. You . . . you've been crying, you know. Sometimes people have—they have thoughts and they know they're wrong, so they feel bad and—"

I laugh because what Ray does is not thought. It is action, creation, destruction; a whole word that he rules. Five years have not been full of thoughts. They have been full of him making and unmaking me whenever he wants.

"You think that's funny?" Barbara's voice has gone hard, angry edge like Ray's when his eyes aren't gleaming but disappointed. Little girl full of lies how could you? After all I've done for you. I rub the bruise on my chest, stiff sore muscles cramp, and scream without sound, my mouth closed, my face still. I'm good at doing that.

I'm used to it.

"I'm sorry," I say, hunching into myself, she is not Ray but she is angry, and if she gets angry and takes me away, no one at 623 Daisy Lane will be all right. "I don't—I'm just sitting here. I just want to be left alone."

"Oh," Barbara says, different voice now, softer, and sits down next to me on the bench. "Did you used to be like her, the girl on the swings? Maybe once upon a time? And then maybe your parents—"

Bitter taste in my mouth, like Ray's skin shoving into me—take it, Alice, take it, open wide, that's my girl—and I lean forward, staring down at the ground. Once upon a time was a long time ago and that girl is gone forever.

"I was never like her."

Barbara crosses her legs at the ankles. Her shoes are black, her feet small. "You hungry?"

I sit up because I am, I always am, and she says, "Here," and hands me a sandwich. It is in a plastic bag, and it is big, two huge slices of bread, lots of meat, and not one but two slices of cheese. My stomach cramps so hard my vision spots, and my hands shake when I take it.

"You still have the card I gave you?" Barbara asks as I'm eating and I nod, closing my eyes, pretty sandwich with salty cheese and slippery ham and cottony bread, so light in my mouth. I could eat these forever, until the world ended and beyond.

"You live around here?"

I swallow, think about Ray watching the door with a knife at my throat. This is what he didn't want, doesn't want, and I could tell her everything—I live with a man who says he's my father but isn't my name is Alice but it really isn't five years ago once upon a time I died and now I am here and take me home to 623 Daisy Lane please.

Ray would know. I wouldn't come home and he'd know and leave and 623 Daisy Lane would disappear, the whole house burned and everyone inside dead while the police checked to make sure I was real and they would never find him and when they told me I was safe—and I will never be safe—he'd find me and I'd be a lying woman then.

And I know what he does to them.

"I live over in South Estates," I say, naming an apartment complex at the far end of the other bus line, the one I never ride on. I see ads for it, though, red brick building in pictures on bus stop benches.

"And you come out here to get away?"

I nod.

"Will you be here tomorrow?"

I nod again, Ray's fury when I tell him, and I will have to tell him, choking my throat so tight I can hardly breathe.

"Good," she says. "See you then."

38

I DON'T KNOW HOW ANNABEL CAN STAY on the swings so long. Ray, right after we moved here, took me to a playground near Shady Pines. I'd expected it to be like the apartment, saggy and old, the grass beaten down and sparkling with shattered glass.

But it was gorgeous. Everything was new and shiny and sturdy, glinting in the sun. A woman who spotted the two of us standing there, Ray telling me to go play and me looking at him, checking to see if it was a test, sure it was because that's what Ray did when we first moved here, tested me all the time, said the city had just donated it.

"I hope it looks like this for more than a week," she said,

and Ray laughed and I cringed, the shiny metal too new for me. The kids around it, on it, not like me. I was still brand new, but even then I understood they were not like me. They were a test, and one I had to pass. My heart wasn't as hollow then, still beat with soft thumps of hope.

Even so, I didn't swing, and the playground got taken over by taller kids, ones who sat on the swings and smoked and did things under the slides, and if we drove by and saw them Ray never slowed down to look. Was always proud of me for not looking either.

As if I wanted to see. I know what everyone is capable of, the ooze inside. And those kids' embraces just reminded me of what waited for me. What always waited for me.

Ray never looked for playgrounds after that one time. He didn't need them, he said, wasn't like those sweaty-eyed perverts lurking around, hoping to glimpse a flash of child flesh, bend of an elbow, piece of thigh.

"Sickos," he said. "They just want to look. They don't want to take care of someone. Aren't capable of it. Don't know what love really is." Wrinkled his face, shaking his head. "I feel sorry for them. Don't you?"

Hot hand on my head, blessing curse. Love, Ray would say. My special love for my special girl.

Red-faced, pushing, eyes closing, flying open to look at me, oh Alice, oh Alice, my girl.

I look away from Annabel kicking her feet up into the

sky and watch the grass under my feet. Once, on a talk show, this death expert said it's everything underground that makes grass so green. That dead things make the living.

I want to lie down on the bench then, or better yet, on the grass, rest on something living and see if I can hear the dead underneath. But I can't, because then people will look and Ray doesn't like looking, wants me silent, his little ghost girl.

I lean over and touch the grass instead. I have not felt grass in years. Ray doesn't like me getting dirty.

It doesn't feel like much of anything, and I am oddly disappointed, like when the soap operas are taken off so someone important in a tie can talk about things that don't matter because they will never reach me. Ray has me wrapped up tight from the world.

"You lose something?" Jake says, and squats down across from me, touching my fingers in the grass. I slide my hand back, wipe it on my jeans. His hands aren't hot like Ray's but they are longer than mine, bigger. I know what that means.

"You look . . . nice," Jake says, and I look down at myself, in my too-small jeans and strange strained pink shirt, and wonder what I look like to him. "Wanna go to my car?"

I look like what I am. I live so I can be what Ray wants, what he needs, and you can see it if you look hard enough.

You can see that you can make me do anything. Most
people look away, though. They do not want to see what
it is possible to make with hands just like theirs.

I get up and follow Jake to his car. He offers me some
pills and shrugs when I shake my head no, swallows them
down dry. "Fucking school," he says. "I hate it."

"Does your sister hate school?"

"She's six," he says. "She still thinks it's fun." His look
says I have said something stupid, something everyone
should know, and I look down, wait for him to put his
hands on his belt. Must think of something to say. Must
think of words.

He does it for me, clearing his throat, tapping the fingers of one hand against his leg. "You like school?"

"It's okay." I remember desks and telling secrets and
standing in line for lunch. Throwing food away because I
was full or didn't want it.

I would give anything to go back and take that food,
slap that stupid once upon a time girl and shove what she
was too dumb to want down my throat, eat and eat until
I grew thick, fleshy everywhere with rolls protecting me
from everyone's eyes. From Ray's eyes.

"So, uh, do you want to . . . ?" He rubs his leg, and
then tries to take my hand again. I let him this time, hold
still while he rubs it across the front of his jeans. He is so
tentative, so unsure.

He seems so young, younger than I've ever been, even when I was born into Ray's arms, and it takes no time at all for me to talk without words, without doing anything that Ray will see. Just my hand moving back and forth, not even on his skin. So easy.

He tries to touch me afterward, hands on my chest, mouth looming toward mine. He does not push my breasts down, flattening them, but cups his hands around them. I don't mind that, but I do not like his mouth on mine, him trying to breathe into me, the darting slick surface of his tongue. Ray kisses my forehead or my knees or the insides of my thighs, but his mother made him kiss her good night every night and so he told me he'd protect me and never kiss me.

I push away after I've counted to ten twice, and he says, "I don't kiss right, do I? My last girlfriend said I sucked."

I don't know what to say to that, to the naked worry in his voice. His weakness makes me nervous.

It makes me want to hurt him, too.

"See, my friend Todd—you've probably seen him, the really tall guy with the amazing girlfriend, the one with legs . . ." He trails off. "Anyway, he had her set me up with May, who is kind of fat but does it with anyone and—well, we went out for a while. Todd says I shouldn't be such a fucking girl about this stuff but, you know, it's not like—" He blows out a breath. "It's not like there's a fucking manual or anything, is there?"

He laughs. "A fucking manual? Get it? Shit, these pills kick ass. Sure you don't want one?"

I shake my head, and words fall into it. "I have better ones."

"Bet you do," he says. "You're like . . . I don't know. A rock. You know, nothing to see, but then you pick it up and there's this stuff on it. What kind of pills?"

"Where does your sister come in the park?"

"Lucy?" he says. "I don't know. The entrance over by the school, I guess. How come you always ask about her? I'm too boring to talk about?" Ray would say that as a low, throbbing whisper, louder than a roar, but Jake makes it a needy whine, like a fly's buzz.

Bzzzz. Bzzzz. I listen to the flies during the day, in the summer. They fly around, living on who knows what—air maybe?—and then, come fall, they're gone. I wish I could be a fly. Live on nothing. Have wings.

"You do like me, right?" he says. "I did everything Todd said, offered you my best stuff, talked to you, washed up after gym."

I do not know normal, but I do not think Jake is it. He is watching me, huge-eyed, far away but here at the same time. So eager to be told he's good, he's special, that he . . .

He reminds me of me. Living dead boy, all broken inside.

"What happened?" I say, and he blinks slowly, slip sliding in his seat.

"What do you mean?"

"What happened to you?"

He sits up and fingers his belt buckle. There is no bulge under it, though. It's an empty gesture. A trying.

When we first moved to Shady Pines I used to turn to Ray at night, thinking if he thought I wanted his sweat and hands and pain, it would be over sooner, that he'd let me go earlier each night, that maybe he would give me grace.

Grace is my favorite church word. A state of being. Something you can pray for. Something God can grant. Something you can obtain. Perfection is out of reach. But grace—grace you can reach for.

"Nothing," he says. "Well, my parents. Disappointed, you know, 'cause I'm not smart or anything, not good at stuff. I'm like my real dad, who up and ran away."

"But your sister's perfect."

"Your face," he says, blinking like he's asleep and trying to wake up. "You—you look funny when you talk about her. Like you want to eat her, or something. Swallow her up whole." He shakes his head, closes his eyes.

Will he go to sleep? If he does, I could—could I leave now?

I wait one breath, two, twenty. Then whisper his name. "Jake?"

"Want to enjoy this," he says, sullen fly buzz back in his voice. "Not think about things. And you . . . you don't like me at all, do you?"

"No," I say, and watch his eyes fly open, mouth drop into a little round O I could twist my fingers into, knotting his lips before squeezing his jaw. Bending him back, forcing him down. He would do it, I think.

He would break.

I lean over, put my mouth on his. Bite his lip, feel the flesh, soft and tender, caught between my teeth. Hear his startled, slow yelp.

Watch him wipe his mouth when I pull away, no hand raised, no words, no voice. He's just still. Silent.

Just like I sit with Ray. Just like I am when Ray reaches for me.

"Be here tomorrow," I say, and leave. I don't even stop to look at Annabel before I go, just walk to the bus, the taste of his broken mouth in mine.

Now I know why Ray does not care about food, why he eats the same meals over and over, why all the things that cramp my stomach with want mean nothing to him. I am all filled up, head to toe crammed with having Jake sitting there watching me. Those wide drugged eyes, and what was behind them.

Fear.

39

RAY KNOWS WHEN I GET HOME. OF course he knows, senses I have seen what he understands and watches me walk toward him, grinning wide. You did it, Alice, he says, you found out when she's coming back and it's tomorrow, no question in his voice, fact, Ray owns the world, he makes what he wants happen, and I nod yes.

He says, Come here. He says, You're my pretty girl. You're my forever girl. My girl. My Alice.

He pinches the stub of my left breast hard, then grabs the right and hauls me in, face changing, smile shifting into his real one, all gums and teeth. Ready to tear.

He says, Do you see what time it is? He says, Do you know how long I've been here, waiting?

I look at the cable box. 5:02 it says in red, 5:02, and I am supposed to be home before then, I should always be home when Ray gets there, should always be waiting for him and he says—

He says, Do you think you can do this without me, you think you can have some kind of—pause—spit hot on my face—fun? You think some boy is fun?

Shaking me now, my head and neck go SNAP back and forth.

You think you were having fun?

No Ray no I swear I just—

You just what—? Watching my face, thumb tracing my lips, pressing hard.

He won't be a problem I got him to come tomorrow and he will and Annabel will be there, she's all better, he said so, she'll be there waiting and she's so pretty you'll like her Ray you'll love her I'll hold her down, hold her hands while you show her how to behave.

"And that's all?" Fingers in my hair, tearing, pushing me down onto the floor.

"That's all, he's nothing, you know it, I know you know it."

Teeth snapping by my neck. Whisper, *I do. I know everything.*

Now everything is familiar. He says, You need me. You love me. Say it. Say it.

Say it, I have said it, I will say it now. I talk until my voice dries up. Words are just letters, A-L-I-C-E, and I know the ones he wants to hear.

Ray sits me on his lap and gives me sips of water after, crackers and a tiny piece of cheese, a special dinner, the cheese coming from his own food, a sandwich he bought, a large roll with meat oozing out the sides.

Mine, he says, but I'll share it with you. Soft kisses on my tender skin and I look at the ceiling so my flesh won't creep away from him.

He says, Kissing it better, you see? Making you all better. Aren't you better?

I nod. Stare at the ceiling and think that soon Annabel will be here. Soon I will not be alone.

40

ONCE UPON A TIME, THERE WAS A little girl. She took long showers every night, swimming in the water rushing over her and washing her hair till it squeaked when she ran her hands down it, parents sighing why do you have to be so clean?

It was like she knew, in a way. Like that water was grace and soon she would not be able to find it. Soon nothing would make her more than what she was.

Nothing would make her whole.

41

RAY IS READY IN THE MORNING. HE wakes me up early, before the sun is even up, taking me by the hand—circle around the wrist, his fingers overlap my bones easily—to the shower.

"Today's the day," he says. "I want you to look special for our little girl."

He does not want me shaving the hair on my legs or under my arms, other Alice tried something, I think. Ray once talked about red water and Alice's hurt wrists in his sleep, anger waking him up and sending him crush-crashing into me.

Sometimes I think if I could meet other Alice I would hold her head under water myself.

He hands me a cream to use and I stare at its bright label as I smear it on me; strange, strong odor, flowers and something that makes the inside of my nose burn. He would wax me all over but it costs a lot, and Ray believes in saving. Plus my stinging legs and armpits, when smooth, will still never equal the tenderness of the stripped skin between my legs, so what would there be for him to savor?

He does not like to see me with the cream on, does not like the smell or the reminder that my pink nightgown used to drag along the floor, leaving a trail behind me. Now its end rests almost at my knees, and the lace trim that once ran around the collar is worn down, rubbed away by washing and Ray's hands tracing over it. Tracing over me.

He packs while I wait for more bits of me to fall off, and when I am done I wash the smell off and pick up the shampoo after he pounds on the door and says, "And wash your hair too!"

When I am done he checks my hair to make sure it is clean enough, and then has me sit and comb it while he shaves. He talks about the money, which he's already gotten out and packed, the maps he's bought, the places we might go. Nevada. New Mexico. Arizona. Somewhere big enough for him to get a job.

Somewhere that will never notice us, our newness when we come in, our wrongness as we walk around. He tells me what he will do to Annabel and how I will hold her hands and maybe even help him, turning around to hold my hand, stroke my fingers. Shaving cream on his face, a little cut on his throat.

"You'll smell like her," he says, eyes gone far away. "We all will."

I pull the comb through my hair. Ray makes sure I use conditioner so it won't tangle. He says he wouldn't like to cause me any pain.

His mother cut knots out of his hair, scissors leaving tiny silver scars on his scalp. He showed them to me after we came here, after he found me walking down the road toward the highway, thumb out like I wanted a ride.

Two days after we moved into Shady Pines, and I thought, I can't live here. I can't.

He drove me all the way to 623 Daisy Lane when he found me, stopped the truck—brand new, I bought it just for you he said, you were supposed to wait for your surprise and you didn't, now get in. He drove right by the house and told me what he'd do to the people inside.

Then we drove home. He pulled over, Exit 56, I remember the sign, nothing but trees and a closed gas station, and got me out of the truck. Into the woods. Smash crash into the trees, dirt grit bugs twigs in my face, my mouth, my head slamming into the ground over and over again.

His hands in my hair.

His voice. You won't leave me. You won't leave me. You won't leave me. Say it.

I won't leave you.

Not ever?

Not ever.

Back to Shady Pines, and I thought, I can live here. I thought, and then, after a while, I just started watching TV. It made the days pass faster.

Easier.

42

RAY CALLS IN TO WORK, SORRY, FAMILY emergency, sick brother out in Pennsylvania, not in Philly, he wishes, but out west, near Pittsburgh. He practices before he calls, makes me listen.

"Do I sound okay?"

I nod. He calls and then, when he's done, shows me Annabel's new clothes again, ones we had to buy at the thrift store two towns away. (Birthday gift for my cousin, I was supposed to say if anyone asked. No one did. The man in front of us bought six faded ladies' bras and an old television set, wood-paneled with a huge number pad worn down from someone pushing in channels.)

We bought old clothes, jeans with pink trim on the

pockets, elastic waist and boxy shape. Nothing like the jeans I've seen shopping with Ray lately, the kind that curl in at the waist and push out at the hips, no more girls' section for me, salespeople saying, "Oh, they do grow up so fast now, don't they?" and Ray's mouth twitching, then buying me boy's jeans. Narrowing his eyes at home as I hold my breath and tug them into place.

Smiling as they slip over my hips. Still in kids' clothes, little girl playing at being a boy.

Come over here and let me see. Let me see my little Alice.

Ray went a little crazy with the shirts, tiny tanks and tees, blouses with lace and shiny white buttons shaped like pearls. Skirts too, little ones with flippy bottoms, flounces for him to toss up.

New underpants bought at the big store where we buy toilet paper and the cleaner I use to mop the floor, white only, no lace, no trim, smaller than mine. Smaller than mine, Ray noticed, and no dinner for me that night.

Sneakers with pink shoelaces, we bought those too. Ray was sure he knew her size.

"I'm good at guessing," he said. "I'm good at knowing what will be just right. Who will be." A smile for a little girl, red-haired, freckled, looking at sandals near us.

Girl smiled back. Ray went over to look at shoes with her, oh I have a little girl about your age, no she isn't here she's home sick, hold out your leg so I can see the shoe, yes I think I like that, I do. Come on, Alice.

Pulling over on the way home, empty construction site, abandoned office building. So eager it is over in seconds.

"I wish all little girls could be like that," Ray said. "Stay like they are forever. Never grow up into what they all become."

Pointing at a woman struggling with the hands of two little girls at the bus stop, angry-faced and exhausted-looking, quick smack one, two, on the back of the girls' heads.

"Who could hurt a child like that?" he says. "Someone should report her. I hope someone does. Children should be loved. They are love."

43

AFTER THE WOODS, AFTER I TRIED TO hold out my hand for a way back to 623 Daisy Lane, Ray carried me to the truck. "See this?" he said, and parted his hair with his fingers, showed me long silvery lines on his scalp. "My mother did that. Cut me when my hair got dirty, cut me trying to get the tangles out. If I'd done a better job, she wouldn't have had to do it."

He drew my hand, paper limp and smeared with dirt, to his head. "I don't want to be like her," he said. "I won't be like her. But I will have to punish someone if you can't be good. And you want to be good, don't you?"

Oh yes I said yes I will be good please let's just go home

don't take me back there again I want to go home with you now.

He smiled. Ray's smile is wide and sunny, happy.

Rotten, dead inside, underneath.

When I smile, I think it looks like his.

44

AS I'M WATCHING THE MORNING TALK shows, Ray is mapping out roads, maps open all across the kitchen table, and I realize I will not see this apartment again. Goodbye singing refrigerator.

Nothing else is worth thinking about, and I go back to watching people yell at each other. Today men who didn't know they were dating men who were pretending to be women are screaming they were tricked, they aren't like that—that way, they keep saying, I'm not that way.

I wonder what TV will be like in the desert, if the channels will be in the same place or if I will have to learn everything again.

Annabel will cry a lot. She will say she is Lucy. She will want to go outside. She will talk about her parents. Her brother.

Maybe I will tell her that I know him. That he hated having to pick her up. That he used to have me do something Ray will teach her how to do. That everyone will think he's the reason why she's gone.

I will have her bring me water. I will eat her food. Help her stay little for longer than I did. Take her to the pool and let her swim.

If she tried to sink, to bury herself in the water, would I let her?

No. I would drag her out. Make her breathe. Take her back to Ray. And then, one night, when he is with her, I will run. I will run and I will—

I forgot. I forgot my plan. A strange rusty noise comes out of my mouth, sharp like a knife. Ray looks up, eyes narrowed, and I point at the TV.

"Shouldn't watch that trash," he says. "It's not funny, other people's pain."

I nod. Yes, Ray. Yes.

I laughed? Is that what that sound was?

I feel so light inside. Like I could float away.

I forgot my plan but I have a plan. I will leave Jake to get in trouble and Ray will have Annabel and 623 Daisy Lane is . . .

I will find it. I will buy a map if I need to. Gas and a map and a package or three of those snack cakes with the filling that oozes out of the sides.

Ray touches my face. "Going to the park," he says. "See you soon."

I nod, and he pinches my jaw.

Yes, I say. Yes. See you soon.

He smears a thumb over my neck, pushing pressure, but then kisses my forehead and leaves. Off to wait for Annabel. Come into the park, come into his waiting arms.

Alone, I stand up, and the room tilts crazily. I see my breakfast yogurt still sitting on the table. Last night's is there too. A note, written in Ray's long, slow scrawl, says he is proud of me. Says I look beautiful. Next to it is exact change for the bus.

Nothing is in the fridge. It's empty, cleaned out, and I think of the tiny piece of cheese, my special dinner, and how far I have to go today. All I have to do.

I have to eat.

I go down to the laundry room, the walls closing in and out and in and out, and go through the pile sitting on top of the third washer. I find matches, a quarter, and bits of fuzz. I lean my head against the dryer. Warm ka-thunk ka-thunk against my head.

The only other pile of clothes is one that belongs to the

old man who lives under the stairs across from the laundry room. He only ever eats soup and talks endlessly about how poor he is to Ray, who is always in a bad mood after he runs into him.

His clothes smell like unwashed old man, like Ray sometimes does in the morning, and my stomach does a little churning flip as the walls close in and then go back out again.

There is fifty dollars in the old man's pants, tucked into the pocket. Wrapped around it is a grocery list. Types of soup and toilet paper.

I clutch the money in my hand. I walk upstairs. I walk outside.

I walk across the street to the fast-food restaurant Ray sometimes brings food home from, burgers and fries that he eats while telling me about his day or after I have told him how much I missed him. (Show me, he always says. Better show me. My knees are always bruised.)

I order a #2 meal, a two-patty burger with cheese and lettuce and a secret sauce. The container of fries is larger than my hand, and my soda is tall, icy cold in a paper cup.

I eat slowly, because I know I have to at first. But not for long, it doesn't take long, not like in those movies I sometimes watch when the soaps are bad, ones where women cut or starve themselves and eventually learn to be strong, but the first steps are so hard, their unbroken skin making them sick, a normal meal making them vomit.

I am so hollow there is nothing inside to be pushed out. I eat slowly for half the burger, meat cheese bread exploding on my tongue, then faster, faster.

I want more food but I can wait. Ray will not find the money. Ray will not find me. He will have Annabel and I will go to 623 Daisy Lane and make them leave, tell them I'm sorry but they aren't safe, I tried, I did, but I don't want to do it anymore, don't want to be Alice, living dead girl, anymore.

I will eat in the car on the way there; buy things I see people eating when Ray and I stop to buy gas on the way home from the grocery store every Saturday. Hot dogs and oozy snack cakes and tiny pizzas in a cardboard box. Chips with a well of bright yellow cheese sauce.

I dream, eyes open, all the way to the park.

Annabel is gone when I get there, and on the swings, where she should be sitting, is Ray.

And he is talking to Barbara.

45

I WANT TO RUN BUT I CAN'T, I CAN'T. I tried and it didn't work, it never works, every day I am an open sore, a walking scream, and it doesn't matter.

No one sees me.

I want to run, but I know there is nowhere I can go.

46

BARBARA SEES ME AND WAVES. MOTIONS
me over. I go, feet moving, always moving to
where Ray is. He is watching, smiling easily, and
I know I must be careful. I must do what he wants.

Knife at my throat as we waited the day the cop came
by. Don't want to don't want to don't want to, he'd whispered. But no one else can have you. I don't want you
broken.

"Hey there," Barbara says. "How you doing today?"

I shrug, sullen child, like I am supposed to when people
ask questions Ray doesn't want me to answer.

"Good," she says. "That's good. Any more trouble with
your brother?"

Shrug again. Don't look at Ray. Don't look to see if he's mad. He will be if you look. My plan, car run food, is still thump bumping around in my head. Will he see it? Did he see it?

"You look a little . . . healthier too," Barbara says, and looks at Ray. "This is the girl I was telling you about."

"Oh," Ray says. "I hope you kept the card she gave you. Hope you know there are places—people—who will take care of you."

"I lost it," I say, still not looking at him, but he is mad, he is furious, I hear it in the honey of his voice, and Barbara says, "I have another one," and hands it to me.

"Well, Ray, I'll take you up on that walk to my patrol car now," she says. "I can do some paperwork, catch up on everything. Love the all-day school field trips, that's for sure."

"The park is lovely like this," Ray says. "Very quiet," and walks right by me, Barbara at his side.

I lied and he knows it, she wasn't out sick he will figure it out sick girls don't go on field trips she should have been here but she isn't and he will know he will find the money 623 Daisy Lane is four hours away he has a knife and will use it and it will be all my fault.

I turn, blind staggering for the bus stop because I have to try and stop him say I am sorry say I will be the best girl ever I will do more than hold Annabel down I will show her what to do, teach her everything while you watch, all the things you want. Anything you want.

Hand on my arm, he has come back for me, he doesn't care who sees, the park is so quiet, he'll take me to the truck, drive away back to where a little girl once lived and I can't stop him, could never stop him, turn and say, "Please, don't. Don't go to them. Just be mad at me."

"What?" Jake says.

47

"NOTHING," I SAY. "NOTHING. WHAT are you doing here?"

"You said to be here," he says. Cracking voice, tone I know. His eyes are already heavy-lidded, dazed. I wonder how many pills he would need to get through my day.

"Your sister isn't here."

"Yeah, she's at some museum or something. Have to pick her up at school at six, and then she'll want to come here and since she always gets her way I'll have to do it."

"She'll be here? Later?"

"Yeah. Why do you care? Hey, why is that guy watching us? Why is he—he's staring right at you."

I don't have to look to know it's Ray. To guess what Ray is thinking.

"Go away," I tell Jake, mind racing 1, 2, 3, I can fix this, I have to fix this, "but come back later. Meet me later."

"I don't—why?" he says. "Hey, that guy is really sort of—I mean, the way he looks at you, it's like you and him are . . ." His voice trails off, surprise shock blooming on his face, in his eyes.

"Are you?" he says, his voice rising on those words. ARE YOU?

Oh I see his eyes, I see what he thinks he knows. He sees but doesn't.

He sees: I am one of those girls, hooking up with an old guy, finding a daddy figure to love cuddle them give them gifts make them crazy using boys like Jake, but it doesn't matter now, not now; yes, I say Yes I am with him but I have to get away from him, you can help just be here tonight, just be here and—

"Save you?" he says, taking one step back, then another. "You're—holy shit. You're serious."

Bring your sister, I was going to say. Bring your sister.

But that is what will save me.

I feel Ray watching me. Judging me. Alice, Alice, Alice, you lied to me you aren't my little girl you have to be punished why do you make me do these things? They hurt me so much more than they hurt you.

"Please," I say to Jake, "please be here, just you and your sister be here, right here, I will be here and—"

"And I'll stop him," he says, weird scared happy expression twitching across his face. "You want me to stop him."

He can't, there is no way he ever could. How can he not see that? But I don't say that, just watch his eyes. Watch feelings cross like shadows, pity understanding horror lust.

Broken girls will do anything, and in the end, that's what he sees. They are empty inside, and nothing can fill them.

But they will let you try.

"I'll be here," he says, and grins, standing up taller, dreaming. "I'll get you and when he comes and everything goes down, then we'll see . . ." Words trail off, I watch him dream like a once upon a time little girl used to. Big dreams.

Impossible dreams.

He can't stop Ray. Nothing can. Nothing will. But the plan will work now. The plan will still work.

"Yes," I say, and force myself to touch his arm, sliding my hand across his skin like he's Ray, like I must do to show Ray how much I love him, how glad I am that he takes care of me. "Yes, you can fix everything. Tonight."

I think he will want to go home and dream but he is not a once upon a time little girl, he knows what I can do, what I am, and wants it, wants it.

"Can you—come to the car, okay? Tonight, I'll protect you, I swear."

Lie. I see his boy eyes, and saving me is nothing to him. Glory for himself, maybe making it so his sister can never play here again. Look at what almost happened to you. Look at what the world can do. That's what he'll say to her.

In the end, he will leave me to Ray, to his anger, but he does not understand that Ray knows about him. Needs him.

"I'll protect you," he says again in the car, and I see him wondering what it's like. What I do with Ray. What he does with me. "How'd you hook up with the old guy, anyway? You don't think you love him or some shit like that, do you? But me, maybe you could. Right?"

"Yes," I say, and try not to think of Ray and how furious he is, how furious he will be, how he will be waiting, waiting.

"Yes, me?" he asks, swallowing down another two pills as he fumbles with my clothes, with his, with a condom.

"You," I say, just a word, just a nothing, like this, like him.

You, Ray. You, Jake. You You You. Alice/I will always pick you.

Alice/I will always be whatever you want. It's what she/I was made for.

It's all I know how to do.

48

LEAVE JAKE DAISY-EYED, DARK PART OF HIS eyes huge like flowers that grow on the side of the road, little yellowing always dying petals with huge black centers.

Ray is waiting over to the side, walks away when I head toward him but manages to be my shadow to the bus stop, shadow so big shadow, mouth grim. Watches when I get on the bus.

Wait for everyone to get on, wait for the transfer bus to arrive, for everyone that wants to get on to do so, struggling with bags and flesh and exact change only.

See Ray's truck behind us when we pull onto the road.

On the bus I sit numb, one stop two stop three stop four, people getting on and off. Some with bags, groceries, work, huge purses that hold tiny phones. Two girls, giggling with pink glossy mouths, get on and sit in front of me.

Shit He Totally Likes You

You Think?

Yes WhatWillYouDo?

Don't Know? Call Him? DoICallHim?

YeahDoItNow

OhMyGodCan'tWaitTillNextWeekWhenIGetMY CAR

I wish I had a car

CallHim!

Someone coughs; the bus way to say shut up, and they SIGH, turn to each other and whisper.

Don't see Ray's truck anymore but I know it's there.

The girls are babies, little girls like the once upon a time one used to be, but they are wiser too. The world did not, will not, eat them whole. They talk all the way to their stop, Call Him, Okay But What Do I Say, Just Call Him. No coughing can stop them.

Everyone breathes happy when they get off. I watch them walking away, strange beautiful girls. No wonder Jake wants my skin. Girls like them would look right through him.

My stop. Stand up, walk. Through the windows, large plastic pieces, smeared, I see nothing but Ray, standing by where I will touch the ground.

Waiting.

49

THIS IS MY FAVORITE STORY. I USED to tell it all the time, whisper it in my brain over everything. Ray always shoved through it though, hot hands pushing me, pulling me, stretching me out. He never heard my story but he taught me it wasn't true. It was just pretend but pretending is hard.

Easy was turning on the TV and watching its endless stories. Letting it tell me tales that ended with songs for toilet cleaners or cars. Watching Ray's face until everything was a blur, past fearangerhate into nothingness.

This is the story:

Once upon a time, there was a girl. She lived at 623 Daisy Lane. Her parents were named Helen and Glenn and she had a room with blue walls. She had a computer and a desk and nail polish that she could wear to school.

She would put on eye shadow in the school bathroom with her friends. Blue to match her eyes.

She was almost ten, and right before her birthday she got sick and had to stay home and missed the big trip to see the aquarium but her friends said it sucked and there weren't any dolphins and her parents said she never ever had to go there.

She had her party and ate cake and ice cream and then—

And then—

And then that's where the story ended. Even then, in the beginning, when I tried to pretend, I couldn't. Nothing waited for that girl after she missed her trip. Nothing I could see past her room and her parents and they didn't fade, never faded, but froze, never moving. What had been became what was and a story only works when you know the ending.

When the people in it don't seem like pretend. When you can think about that girl and how she was once upon a time, and see her.

When you don't already know the story is a lie.

50

R AY TAKES MY ARM AS I STEP OFF THE
bus, hand around the upper part of it, smiling
at the other person getting off, tired-looking
woman with straining plastic shopping bag, can poking
through a ripped corner. Green label. Vegetable.

Vegetables always have green labels. In the supermarket
I stare at all the food, peanut butter goes with jelly, bread
is with the coffee, vegetables across from pasta in its red
or white boxes.

"Let's get you home," Ray says. "I've been worried
about you, wondering where you were. You should have
told me you were going out. Here, take my hand. You
look tired."

No one is listening, bus gone, chemical burning smell of it drifting over us, woman clutching her bag and heading down the sidewalk.

To the apartment, Ray's hand clamped claw over mine. Four small separate buildings, sixteen units in each one. Once I spent part of the morning figuring how many there were, remembering school and how I hated to sit in my seat and do my work and do my homework, learn, learn, learn.

I remember so little. Stripped down to bare flesh breathing to stay alive. Say I love you. Say I want to be with you. Say thank you for taking care of me.

Be good and everyone at 623 Daisy Lane will be safe.

We live in complex two, over to the right, down into the parking lot, dip that collects water when it rains, then up past the ground down grass where girls sometimes stand talking to boys, Ray catching glimpses of them out the window and shaking his head. That's what women do. How it all starts. Scratching his back through his T-shirt like the scars there still burn.

He talks all the way there, so worried about where you were, so worried about how tired you look, what about your schoolwork, hope you did it, don't want you falling behind, you have to learn things.

You hear that? You have to learn.

Ray's voice is so steady my skin starts to shrivel. Ray has to work on talking like this not LIKE THIS because he gets upset easily the world is not a good place it's full of bad things and people and it bothers him but he works on it, works on it. At work he says people call him Silent Ray because he's so quiet and he likes that it's better than Fat J or Pepperoni D or Assy the Clown, which is what everyone but Ray calls Harold, their boss. Ray says names are important. You don't give them away.

Inside he pushes me away like my skin hurts him and I spin across the carpet, caught before I can fall because his fist catches me, slams into my chest. Into the bruise that hasn't healed, right by where the knot that is my heart beats.

I gasp, pain so familiar. Welcome, come in. It will be okay. Ray angry like this is familiar. I drop to my knees and wait for the hands in my hair. Yank me forward or push me back. I will say what you want me to.

Ray does not touch me. Circles around me, frowning, then walks into the kitchen.

What to do? What do I do?

Follow, crawling, pain in my chest, red hot breath burns.

On the kitchen table Ray is opening a box, taking things out: Knife. Matches. Rope. Map. Paper with 623 written on it and boxes for all the rooms. Labeled. Kitchen. Dining Room. Living Room. Study. Helen and Glenn's room. Baby's room.

ALICE's room with a big X through it.

"I'd gotten everything packed," Ray says. "We were supposed to be on the road by now. Going to the desert. But you—" He shakes his head. "You. Look what you made me go and get."

Won't even look at me. Just touches the paper, 623 Daisy Lane, tracing over the rooms. The names.

"Sorry," he says to it, to them. "I tried, but Alice wasn't good at all. She'll tell you she was when you see her but you'll know she's a liar."

He picks up the knife and I am pinned in place, watch as he turns it over and over, then hits the air with it. Push, push, push.

"I thought about this," he says. "I thought about it a lot, while I waited, but you would just make the knife dirty and it's a good knife and I want it to stay clean. And you did promise that you'd be good for me. For them. For all of us. Didn't you?"

I nod because I did, I promised in blood and tears and words and curled up and down and around in all the ways he liked. I nod because he has the map and he can't use it, he can't go there, they don't deserve this. Don't deserve him.

"But," he says, still talking, still not looking at me, still slashing the air so hard sweat blooms on his forehead, his eyes going like Jake's, all daisy-eyed and far away. "I'll bring it anyway. Best to be prepared."

Grins at me then, looking at me now, and I think of how they found first Alice, dead in the river.

Her parents died after her funeral, robbery gone bad, nothing taken but they were both stabbed over and over before the house was burned down. Burglar got away with nothing but the article he made me read said TRAGIC END TO SAD STORY.

Burglar never got caught.

For five years I have been good so they can live, for five years I have worked so hard to keep him from driving to 623 Daisy Lane and going inside.

Take me home, please, I once said to him, and he said, You don't want me to do that.

You don't ever want me to do that.

51

"RAY," I SAY, "RAY," AND I SAY:

Ray please don't I swear I thought she'd be there I didn't lie about her being there Jake said she would be and he just forgot I wouldn't lie to you I wouldn't do that I was there too why would I be there if I lied I should have told you about the cop but I didn't want you to worry—

Hand in my hair then knife at my throat.

"You didn't want me to worry? You know, she asked me if I knew you? How would she even guess something like that?"

My whole world is his glittering eyes. His voice, quiet. "How stupid do you think I am?"

138

Knife, sharp pressure against my skin.

No Ray I say no please no I never told her anything she gave me a sandwich you know how cops are they ask questions and she thinks I have no home and maybe thought I ran away and you were taking care of me—

PAIN red hot on my throat.

Because you do take care of me, Ray, you do, and she could probably tell you were careful and would take care of someone and wanted you to know that you could tell she liked you everyone likes you and when I went to Jake I made sure he—

He sticks the knife in my shoulder and I scream.

Silence and then I am swaying, no words for what it's like. I thought living dead girls couldn't feel pain, thought I was emptied out but I'm not, I'm not.

Ray please Ray I love you he's bringing her to the park tonight Annabel will be there tonight I told him (don't say his name, don't say it, that's what made my shoulder scream, blood beating in it like a heart, thump-pain-thump-pain) I would see him he hates her and wants her to go away I can tell he will be there she will be there we can get her—

Knock on the door, and "Shut up," Ray hisses, grabbing my jaw and squeezing it, all the words I was going to say, my plan my stupid plan I forgot and then remembered and the food I ate and the money still in my pocket, all the words in my mouth he squeezes closed.

Room swirling, everything feels so far away.

"Yes," I hear Ray say and I am leaning against the wall, propped on my left side like a broom. I can see the knife handle. Blood red everywhere, down my shirt, on the floor. "Yes, that was my daughter. She was making a salad and cut herself, no, I already called an ambulance but you know how traffic is so I'm driving her there now. Thank you."

PAIN.

Knife on the floor, I see it, it's not in me, but Ray's fingers are there, are digging into me, dragging me up.

"Shut up and put this on," he says, handing me his old shirt, the one he wears when he fixes his truck, smells like him and car, and then box under his arm we go down the stairs and into the truck and then out onto the road, gone.

The highway is exactly 2.3 miles from the apartment. Ray told me this when we moved in and said to remember it. 2.3 miles was all he had to drive to get on the road that leads to 623 Daisy Lane.

"What time is the boy bringing Annabel?" he says.

"When she gets back," I gasp, watching as the highway sign comes closer, closer. "Six. He said six."

Ray turns, and we leave the highway sign behind.

52

H E TIES MY ARM UP WITH ONE OF his old shirts, ripping it open along the side. "You gotta be strong to do something like this. Did you know that? I'm very strong."

I know you are, Ray. You were stronger than me when I followed you into a parking lot. You are stronger than me now.

"Annabel will be safe with you," I say. "So much safer than she is now."

"Does it hurt?" he says, touching my shoulder, and when I nod because it does and because I know his questions, he sighs and says, "Good. I'm sorry, but you . . . You've really disappointed me, Alice. Now, you make it up to me tonight, and we'll just go straight to the desert. Deal?"

He is lying. Ray lies to everyone—at work, at church, when you look at him on the street and see just another guy. But he does not lie to me. I have seen inside him because I come from him. He created me, and now he is talking to me like he talks to them. To everyone else.

"Please," I say, because I know he is lying, there is no deal, there is only what he wants, has always ever been only what he wants with no bargaining, no questions, and he smiles at me, his real smile, all pain and teeth and knowing. We drive to a shopping mall that was built but died, empty stores everywhere with only one sad supermarket at the far end.

"Start making it up to me now," he says, and pushes my face into his lap. Digs his fingers into my shoulder hard.

I hate him. Thought comes like pain and throbs there, screaming. I hate him, hate him, hate him.

I'd forgotten how much feelings hurt.

53

"WHO ARE YOU?" WAS THE FIRST thing Ray said to me after the aquarium, was the first time I heard his real voice.

"Who are you?" he said, and hit me when I answered, slap across my face, my parents had never hit me before, made me sit in a corner when I was bad and yelled, my mother's face sometimes turning bright red and scaring me.

But not like this.

"Who are you?" he said again. "What's your name? Where do you live?" and he didn't know who I was, how could he not know who I was when I was in his car and he—I had words for what he'd done then, words from the

143

news and from talks at school, but how could he not know me? They never said I would be nothing to him, just some stupid girl who said yes, show me where to go.

"Stop crying," he said as I told him, and I did. I sniffed all the tears back up into my head, hiccupped held them in my throat and told him who I was and where I lived.

He nodded. "Good," he said. "Very good."

"Will you take me home?" I said, and he looked at me like I'd asked the silliest question in the world.

"Of course," he said. "Where else would we go?"

"But—" I didn't want him in my house, did not want him near my things, didn't want him with my parents.

"Oh, you mean the other place," he said. "623 Daisy Lane. I could take you there, but then you'd say I hurt you—"

"No, no, I wouldn't, I—"

"I'm talking," he said, and hit me again. It hurt more the second time. "Good girls are quiet when grown-ups talk. Can you be quiet?"

I nodded.

"Better," he said. "Now, I can't take you to 623 Daisy Lane unless you want everyone there to die. Because that's what will happen if you go there. Do you want that? What—" He leaned over and pinched my jaw shut, back then his hand could cover it like it was nothing. "What kind of girl are you?"

Disgust was thick in his voice and when I didn't say anything he said, "I see," and shook his head, and then said, "I guess we'll go, then," and I said, "No, no, I'll go with you."

"You'll come home?"

"I'll come home," I said. And that's when I knew I never would, that home was now just a word, that it meant nothing.

I felt what loss was then, and it was like dying.

It was dying, and when Alice was born, that little once upon a time girl, that far away long ago me, disappeared.

She became a story, one I have mostly forgotten. One I can't end because she died a long time ago.

54

RAY IS ALMOST NEVER HAPPY. YOU would think he would be, he says I make him happy, but I don't. I'm always doing something wrong.

But now he is happy and buys chicken from a fast-food place, leaving me in the truck, whistling under his breath as he comes back jingling his keys and carrying two bags smelling of meat and salt and bread, all warm, soft, good smells.

"After five already," he says, looking at his watch and frowning, wipes spots off it, dried brown-red spots, my blood. Uses the hand cleaner he always carries—germs are bad, his mother taught him, and he is full of them, the world is full of them, and he used to never want me to get sick—and then eats his chicken.

"Here," he says, and puts a biscuit on my knee. I can't pick it up with my right hand and he is holding my left and when I look at him he giggles, high-pitched.

I am scared. I thought I knew fear, lived inside it, breathed it in every day, but this is terror, his laugh and knowing he is going to have me help him take his Annabel and then kill me. Then kill everyone who lived with the girl I used to be.

And he knows I know that. I did not see it before but I see it now. He sees I see my own death and he is keeping me with him because he likes it. He wants to see me waiting for it.

I lean over and eat the biscuit, one bite before it falls off my knee and onto the floor. Ray says, "You're like that cop, that fat cow cop, who ate candy when we were walking back to her car. Women shouldn't eat candy, it makes them fat and all those bulges are horrible. My mother used to wave hers around, I bet that cop does that and I said I'd call her and got her number and when she asked about you I said you needed someone to take care of you and I hoped whoever loved you would do that."

He laughs again and takes a bite of chicken, ripping flesh between his teeth, all the way down to the bone.

55

5:40.

We are close to the park. Ray has finished his chicken and cleaned his hands and pressed my face down into his lap again, then changed his mind and moved me around, folding me into what he wanted, my head pushing into the door as he pushes into me, grunt (him) thunk (me).

"You. Remember. Who. You. Belong. To," he says. "You. Remember. Whose. Girl. You. Are."

I nod and he pushes my hair out from where it has gotten trapped under me, caught by him and how he's moved me.

"There," he says. "That must feel better."

It does, of course it does, not feeling bits of my hair strain, snap. My head goes thunk again, once, twice, and then he sighs. Flexes his fingers on my shoulder, red pain silent scream inside me.

Tears on my face, I cannot help it, and he licks them off one by one, sucking every last thing he can from me.

56

R AY AND I LIVE IN THE TOWN OF CEDAR
Hills. There's a sign and everything. I see it on
the TV channel that runs town meetings and
school lunch menus. I sometimes watch to see what little
girls get to eat.

If you saw Cedar Hills, you would like it. It is a nice
town, with good schools and low crime and tourists
who come to look at the vacation home of a man who
helped write some sort of treaty and a company that
makes expensive tiny phones that you see people talking
on in television shows. So many new houses are going
up that it's like there are ghost towns all around, pockets
where the skeletons of homes sit, waiting to be finished,

waiting for their families to come and move in.

"Now we're ready," he says, and hauls me up, buckles my seat belt around me. Ray insists on seat belts in the truck. He says you can't be too careful with all the other drivers out there. He says it's better to be safe than sorry.

It is strange how slow time has gotten, each minute creeping by. I thought that everything ending would be quick—and I have thought about it every day for five years, thought about it ever since he pulled me close, like a parent putting an arm around a child, and then whispered what would happen if I said anything, if I tried to run, if I said a word.

He said I would be sorry, that I would die, that everyone would die, and Ray always keeps his word.

"Can you—?" I say, my head swimming as my shoulder throbs softer, duller red now, everything getting heavy, my shirt pressing down on me. Empty ghost houses all around us.

"Can I what?"

"Just do it now," I say. "Just kill me. Put me in a house, get the knife, the matches, and—"

He leans over and kisses my cheek. "You do what you're told," he says, and then backhands me so hard I feel something snap crack, feel some of my teeth wiggle up and around, loose.

"You keep your promises to me," he says. "You do

what I tell you to. You remember whose girl you are."

"Yours," I say, "yours," and swallow the blood in my mouth. It is warm, salty.

"Mine," he says, and whistles as we drive away.

57

5:50.

Ray tells me what I will do. I will go into the park. I will find Jake. I will give him whatever he wants and a special purple pill that Ray hands me, tells me to make sure Jake takes. I will wait until he has drifted far away, eyes wide shut.

Then I will walk by Annabel. I will stop if there are other children with her. ("And there will be," Ray says. "On a night like this, who wouldn't want to be out playing?") I will pretend to tie my shoe so Ray will know he has to come a few minutes later and tell everyone the park is closing early, sorry, town rules, things have to be painted like that statue at the far end so go on, go find your parents. Go on, go home.

Annabel will head for Jake and find me.

And then Ray will come for us. "Right there, at the boy's car," he says, and grins, laughs, "I know what you were thinking," in a singsong voice, teasing like the kids I saw pushing smaller ones around, grinding them down into the ground.

"You leave when I say," he says. "You leave with me. You don't get to be alone with the boy like that. With his car."

Laughs again. "It'll be good for Annabel, I think. See what happens to her brother. Start her off right to see what happens when you don't listen. I wish I'd done it with you. But between that and our trip to Daisy Lane—no, I didn't forget—she'll learn what she has to do. She'll learn to be good."

"I'll run," I say, slow, sluggish, the words like weights in my mouth and Ray looks at me like he has never seen me before, like I am someone—something—new.

Then he laughs and pats my face, not a slap, but a pat, fond soft rubbing, his hot hand on my face.

"No," he says. "You won't."

And he is right. I won't. Not because I don't want to, but because I can't. Because my shirt is so heavy now, hard weight on my skin, and I feel strange, hot and floaty and weirdly sleepy, darkness pressing in against me like Ray at night turning to loom over me.

Unstoppable.

That's what night is. What Ray is. And I am nothing against any of that. Against him. I never have been.

Little Alice, all hollowed out, so easy to smash into a million pieces.

58

I HAVE BEEN SMASHED AND PUT BACK together so many times nothing works right. Nothing is where it should be, heavy thumping in my shoulder where my heart now beats.

Feel it? Pushpushthrob, one beat. Pushpushthrob, two beats.

Now, Ray says. Now.

59

"Now," HE SAYS AGAIN AND LEANS across me, unbuckling my seat belt, opening the door. 6:02.

Pushing me out.

I do not fall. I fell so hard so long ago there is nothing left for me to land on. I just keep falling and falling and falling.

My shoulder-heart throbs and I walk, still falling.

Into the park, over to where the cars are, not by the lights or the shiny slides and swings.

To Jake's car, empty. I look in the window, try the door. It opens, smell of boy and sadness and handfuls of pills. I lean inside, head spinning, beyond dizzy, world tilting swirling melting running into dark, and then pull back. My shirt drips onto his seat, plop plop plop, blood like tears because both do nothing except make Ray happy or sad you never know with him what kind of mood he's in and I used to think I could figure them out, be what he wanted, but it was never right I was never right.

And in the end blood and tears are alike because they stop too. You can't have either go on forever. You will go on—I did, I am, get up, day goes by, Ray comes home, nighttime, bed, sleep to wake up and do it all over again over and over and over like we pray in church, world without end.

Amen.

60

I HEAD BACK TO THE PARK. JAKE IS probably there, waiting in the bushes or behind a tree, thinking he will do something, but instead will just be there, daisy-eyed watcher that Ray will smash if he finds.

It is hard to see in the dark, the lights faint far away tunnel shadows, and I round a corner, the left-turning one that marks the curve where the park starts, grass green in the day but now inky dark, reflecting the night.

Annabel is there. She puts her hands on her hips, like a grown-up, head tilted to one side, and I was never this young, not ever.

I wait for her to playact, ask where's my brother at and

sigh like the children at the apartment do, where's my sister at, where's my brother at, where's glenda/maria/shanda/levonda/najari/tedanna at? Ray sometimes watches them, sneaking peeks out the window, me kneeling between his legs as he whispers what he would like to do to them, what he could teach them, how good he could make them be.

Instead she says, "You're bleeding."

61

STANDING THERE, BLACK PANTS, WHITE shirt, orange sneakers (left shoelace untied), she wrinkles her mouth like a grown-up, like the woman she will never get to be, Ray won't let her grow up, not into this world, never grow up he would whisper to me at night, never grow up. Stay just as you are, Alice.

Swear you'll never change. Swear it. Good.

She stands there, staring, and I can see her five years from now, hollowed out, hollow-eyed, shrunken little thing, not a girl but nothing more, not quite right at all but you won't look, will you? No, you will turn away, you will always turn away. Everyone says they want to help but no one really does. He was always so nice, they say on TV about the killer next door. He was so quiet. We never thought there was anything strange about him at all.

The girl? We thought she was his daughter. He said she was sick, that he was trying to get her help. He seemed to be so—well, normal. And she never said a word. Why didn't she say a word? That's all she would have needed to do.

62

"RUN," I SAY, AND SHE BLINKS AT ME. Doesn't move.

Just one word, they say. But no one would listen. I could have screamed a million times in a million voices and no one would have ever heard me. I did, every time I left the apartment, with every step I took out in the world.

All those cries, and no one ever heard them.

Finally, I spoke, I speak, and no one listens. Not even her.

Ray's hand on her arm, he is here now, he heard what I said, her eyes widen but it is too late.

I watch her see what her world will soon be.

63

S HE SCREAMS.

    I didn't. I didn't even think of it, too stupid, too scared, too slow, I was at the aquarium, adults were everywhere my teachers were there all my friends were there my birthday was coming soon I had new lip gloss and the hat I had on was too big, even with my hair shoved up under it and then—

    And then, later, I screamed and no one came. I screamed and no one heard but Ray and he said oh no, no, no, don't do that like he would stop hurting me but then he did and smiled gums bared teeth yellow-white sharp chewing me apart down to the bone.

She screams and Ray shakes her, yanking her forward and back, and her voice cuts off in shock, no one has ever done this to her you can tell no one has ever hurt her no one has ever really shown her what hurt is.

"Let her go." Jake, from the bushes, just like I thought, daisy-eyed, voice slurred.

Gun in his hand.

64

RAY LAUGHS, A REAL LAUGH, THE high-pitched giggle that makes me curl into myself, cringing, and Jake blinks, slow, bewildered, this is his dream, this is the one where he's the hero, and starts to frown. Bad guy isn't supposed to be laughing. Bad guy is supposed to be scared.

See all that, see his thoughts, and Ray knocks the gun out of his hand and then turns his arm slightly, fist into Jake's jaw, nose, smash into his face.

Jake falls to the ground. Eyes open. "Lucy?" he says, "Lucy?" and Annabel starts to cry, tries to twist away. Ray steps on Jake's hand, grinding down the bones, and Jake howls, Annabel wide-eyed looking everywhere and nowhere.

Looks right at me and I feel my heart beat, heavy thud in my chest, slow, so slow, and she sees me, really sees me, living dead girl who she will soon be.

"Come on," Ray says, something in his voice I've never heard before, strange uncertain note, and I open my mouth scream run! For her, for me.

RUN.

She does, slipping little girl fast into the bushes. Ray swears, grabs my shoulder, no messing around now, yanks me around, spins me in front of him like we are dancing, claw into meat, teeth into flesh, and the world roars, shaking the way the sky rattles when thunder comes. My stomach twists like it's opening from the inside, burns like lightning must, my body snapping harder than even Ray can move me.

"You stupid bitch," Ray says, voice emptied out, my death in his eyes, and the world roars again, his fingers sinking deep inside me as his head cracks back, red blossom where his right eye was, staggering forward, crashing down, taking me as he falls, skin blood bone on me, running all over me, running into me.

"Alice," he says, and then again. "Alice?"

Then he is silent, a dark heavy weight on top of me. Pressing me down into the ground. Where all things must go. Where we one day will all be. Death to make the living.

"I did it," Jake wheezes and his face, strange hazy far away, peers at me. "I did it. Two shots but I did it. Where the fuck's my phone? Call the police, call Mom and Dad, call Todd and—Lucy? Lucy? Where are you?"

I want to push Ray off me but I can't move and he is dead, he is gone, and the pain in my stomach is hotter than the one in my shoulder, deeper, and when Jake says my name, phone at his ear, smeared like something melting, he touches my side and lifts up fingers dark like night.

"Oh no," he says, and then "oh no no no" and other words into his phone, hurry I meant to stop him but she moved or something she was there she was with him.

Yes, I was with him. Ten years old and in his car, say yes you will come with me.

Say it.

Good.

I don't have to close my eyes to sleep now it is coming for me I am so tired everything strange, slowed down, quiet, and Lucy—her name is Lucy she will never be called Annabel will never want to forget Lucy is her name. Will be able to keep it.

Lucy kneeling by me, wiggling her hand into mine, little fingers shaking and warm.

"Kyla," I whisper, dark swimming up all around me, filling me up. My name is Kyla Davis I live at 623 Daisy

Lane will you please take me home now? Please?

Yes, Ray said but he didn't he never did he kept me with him keeps me with him still but now—

I don't remember sleeping without him by my side heavy weight pushing me down but now I don't feel him at all, Lucy's hand like a ghost, little voice saying what? What? What did you say?

65

I AM FREE.